Nitrospective

Stories by Andrew Hook

For Sophie:
My Felix, my new world order, my Severine, my cowgirl

Acknowledgements

I would like to thank the following editors for previously
accepting and publishing some of these stories. Their
support is gratefully appreciated.

Allen Ashley, Adam Bradley, Pete Crowther, Trevor Denyer,
Des Lewis, Terry Martin, Ian Millsted, Mike Philbin, Steve
Soucy, Michael Stewart, Sheryl Tempchin, Neil Thomas
and Ian Whates.

Thanks also to Adam Lowe at Dog Horn Publishingand
artist Dean Harkness.

Contents

Nitrospective

She resembles a hare caught in traffic. Beautiful, skittish, terrified, authentic: simultaneously. She's lying on my bed.

Beyond the window is the ocean. If I look out to the horizon that's all I can see.

The line between sky and sea is pretence.

The time for action is past. I have aged. The time for reflection has come.

Faith is on her front. Her naked back bears scars, only some of which are inflicted by me. To add to them is easier than creating marks on unblemished skin. I told her I loved her.

It was the truth. Vérité. Vert. Green.

How simple it is to make links from one word to the other. From one ideal to the other.

Even now I don't know who she is really working for.

*

My orders were to bring her to Southwold for a holiday. The way

Gregory said *holiday* made me shiver, although I kept it inside.

We have information, he said. But didn't reveal it. Because of this, I never knew if I was fighting for the right cause.

But of course, is it possible to fight against a concept rather than an enemy?

Sometimes I wonder why I'm here.

There are some who regard the planes flying into the World Trade Centre as the catalyst. When I saw it, I thought it was performance art.

Thirty years later I am in my mid-fifties. Faith hadn't been born.

If I question my own methods, then I question her ideals even more.

Nothing she has told me makes any sense.

I leave her on the bed and take a walk. What was once a beautified semi-tourist town has become a barricade. Everywhere we are hiding behind barricades, against threats which we can no longer see. Everyone has an enemy, everyone is the enemy.

Seagulls glitter the air. The sky is blue. The light here is fantastic. Magnificently wide and pale. Under a topless sky I sit by the cannons and look out to sea. I'm not worried about Faith. She can't escape when she's tied.

The first time I saw her she was handing out pamphlets. Not political treatise, no one did that any more; it would be tantamount to handing out pieces of paper containing the words *kill me.* Hers were for the new hairdressers in town. People still liked to look good. Her mousy-brown hair framed her face, long at the back, short at the front. When her lips were slightly parted, as they usually were, I could see four of her white teeth. Her blue eyes,

6

accentuated by thick black mascara, were an invitation. I accepted it. She could have been anyone, but I wanted to make her someone.

I wished I could light a cigarette.

The first time I was tortured I immediately told everything I knew. I was respected for that, and enlisted for the other side. When I was captured and subsequently tortured I told everything again. Even now I have no understanding why anyone would keep the truth inside them and accept pain. Let it out, release it. What does any of it matter anyway?

On the bench I wondered whether Faith was holding anything back or whether she genuinely had nothing to tell. I was a calm torturer. I told her my truths and waited for hers. It gave me no pleasure to see her cry. It was like telling someone you loved that you no longer loved them. Which is why I told her I loved her as I marked her supple skin.

Nowhere there is danger. Everywhere there is danger. It all depends on what you believe, and I believe in nothing.

*

Everyone talks about ethnic minorities but no one talks of ethnic majorities.

In 2007 I committed my only political act. On a wall less than two-hundred yards from the American Embassy in London I graffitied a Chad. Familiar half-face, hands, peeping over a wall. Always peeping, semi-hiding. War On Terror. *WOT NO TERROR*. War on terror no terror.

Even as I drew it I was being drawn into it.

I chose allegiances on a whim.

7

Because really none of it made any difference.

It might well be determined that Faith and I are on the same side. Although we won't always have been on the same side and we wouldn't always remain on the same side.

Gregory called me a chameleon. He knew my past which is why he could trust me. You can't trust anyone with ideals. They only do stupid things.

Faith carries a photo of herself in her purse. A full head shot. Maybe she keeps it to retain her identity, to remind herself of how she looked when she takes it out at the point of her death. Outside of her face, the only discernible image is a round ceiling light over her right shoulder. For a while it bothered me that I would never know where that photograph was taken.

Or who took it.

Love does funny things.

I left the bench and continued into town. If I pay attention I remember that the burnt-out husk of a building was once a second-hand bookstore. Pieces of paper aflame would have twirled skywards like reverse sycamores or jigsaw phoenixes. Everything else is much the same. I enter the grocers and buy an apple but even that is a political act.

The apple, of course, is green.

Never give power to someone who doesn't know what they want to do it with.

Never give power to anyone with ideals.

Those without ideals never want power.

I am a pawn.

*

There's a phone box on the corner. Unlike in 2001 when mobile phones were sounding amongst the rubble, calling to the dead, no one carries one any longer. No one wants themselves to be available at any time. Sometimes, listening to a telephone ring in an empty room is solace.

I dialled Gregory's number and waited.

"Anything?"

"Not yet. Are you sure?"

"Can anyone be sure?"

I shrugged. Even though he couldn't see it, Gregory must have known.

"I don't know anything any more."

"You never did. That's why I like you. You're a black screen which refreshes itself every single day. You know it, and you embrace it."

I nodded. "I am essentially passive."

"That's why people like me need you."

"Is there anything else?"

"Just continue."

Gregory's voice was always cool and calm. But underneath I knew that a bear was roaring.

I bought cigarettes for the home, some fruit juice, a couple of microwaveable meals for dinner, a box of matches, an old postcard faded by the sun, a newspaper.

By the time I had walked one hundred yards I had discarded the newspaper.

To my right, as I passed the green outside the pub, a house exploded.

*

"You don't mind that I'm older?"

She shook her head. It was 2029, two years ago.

I touched her breast through her sweater. Even though she wore a bra I could feel the nub of her nipple.

"Have you heard about the New World Order," she said.

"I've always heard of it. It comes around and around and around and has been around since St George killed his first dragon."

She smiled. "But if you look at the proof."

I showed her the proof. NWO. OWN. WON. NOW.

It was only a matter of semantics.

I traced my fingers from her shoulder, along her neck, up to her right ear.

"Language can only be a lie because we expect language to offer explanations. But there are no explanations. There is only what we see."

She took hold of my hand and placed my index finger into her mouth.

"Sometimes there is no need for language."

She said it clumsily. Little girl clumsily. Maybe it was the naiveté which appealed to me. Maybe it was because she was a blank canvas. But more likely it was because I hadn't had anyone for a long time.

Afterwards: "Are you an idealist?"

I shook my head. "An ideal is like perfection. It doesn't exist. All that you can do is fight for it, and all some people want to do is fight."

"Surely you have to fight for what you believe in?"

"And if you believe in nothing?"

Whilst the question hung there I entered her again.

*

I ducked as bricks and tiles flew my way as though on invisible strings, threw myself to the ground as a white picket fence almost speared me. Its tips dug into the grass around me, enclosed me.

There was the usual screaming.

The gulls overhead flew and kept their distance for maybe a minute. Then returned as though looking for the pickings. How easily restoration becomes.

A neighbour emerged from her property. Began shouting about the Arabs, the French, the Germans, the Greens, the Terrorists, the Maoists, the English, the Christians, the Muslims. She shouted about everyone other than herself, but she was just as guilty as the rest of them.

I stood up. Thought of taking out my gun and decided against it. Instead I brushed grass off my trousers, watched as community services arrived and put out the small fire, giving instructions on making the building safe. It appeared that the family hadn't been at home.

In the big scheme of things, for me, that made a difference.

My purchases were in a brown recyclable bag which miraculously hadn't been torn as I threw myself to the ground. Clutching it to my chest, I made my way back to our holiday home.

By the time I reached the cannons, another house had

exploded. Then another, probably. I heard it but no longer looked. If it seemed random and pointless then so did the rest of life. But even then you could just stand there and enjoy it.

There are no puppets. We all have free will.

Some of us choose to be freer than others.

Freedom from choice is what we want, but freedom of choice is what we've got.

Everything is internal.

I walked across the dunes. Even though I wore trousers I could feel the stiff grass whipping my legs. Bending down I pulled up a clump for later, shaking off the sand that clung to it wet at the base.

Rabbit droppings punctuated the landscape. Only man strives for ideals.

When Barack Obama was elected all the wrong people had hope. I thought it was audacious. Within days biographies were on every shelf.

Now even those books don't exist. Expressing an opinion is tantamount to treason.

I ran my tongue around my teeth. One of my gums was bleeding. I couldn't be sure if it was disease or resulted from the blast.

Three hundred yards from the property I reached into my pocket and held the keys. It's always important to be ready. To cross a road diagonally is the fastest angle to get to where you want to go.

The key was stiff in the lock from the rust caused by sea air. I had washed my hair every day that we had stayed. Our relation-ship had become brittle too. Not simply because of the torture, but because I wanted it to be over so I could hold her again.

Faith was as I had left her. I saw an eyelid flicker as I closed the door. She was pretending to sleep. In my absence she had bent her foot back and tried to drag a sheet over her body, but she must have been too weak as her back and buttocks were still exposed.

I sat down on the bed beside her. Ran a finger from the base of her neck to the bottom of her spine.

I had to look away. Tears had filled my eyes. She hadn't shuddered.

Was this what it was all about? Desensitisation? I had maintained my ambivalence because I refused to get involved, saw it as the route to remaining human. Only an idealist could fight the demands of their own body.

I coughed and blood from my mouth speckled her back.

Getting up, I went into the bathroom, poked around with my tongue. Flecks patterned the ceramic when I spat. I filled a glass tumbler with water and rinsed and spat and rinsed until all that I spat was clear.

Through the tiny bathroom window which I always kept open I could hear another explosion.

Back in the bedroom I lay the dune grass on the floor beside the bed. Now it wasn't tethered to the earth it seemed flat, devoid of strength. I probably wouldn't use it unless we made up and she wanted tickling.

"C'mon."

The word fell out of my mouth unbidden. Faith opened one eye.

"Let's just end all this right now. Tell me what you know."

She tried to turn, but her hands which were bound at the

wrist and bound to the bedstead wouldn't allow such a movement.

Her eyes were wet.

I knew that she loved me.

I knew that she had more to tell.

*

Her lips had been full. Particularly the bottom lip. I liked to bite it when I kissed her. I liked her to bite it when she looked at me. Now it was cracked. I stood again, collected the tumbler from the bathroom and filled it with water from the kitchen tap. Holding her head I raised it for her to drink without coughing.

The water restored her voice.

"Bastard!"

I shrugged. I knew it was easy to have no allegiance to any one party or political group or even to any one country, but it was harder to have no allegiance to any one person.

"I've told you. Just tell me what I need to hear and then we can get on with our lives."

"I thought we were getting on with our lives." Her breath came in short bursts. Heartache.

"It doesn't even have to be your truth."

"We've been through all this."

"Don't be an idealist."

"Why? I can see where it got you."

I lit a cigarette.

I could feel her tense, just at that moment. And until that moment I had no intention of putting it on her skin.

When I did, the pain seemed to enter me more than her. I

14

looked around for my medicine.

The nitroglycerin in my angina spray held the same properties that might be found in dynamite. The residue it left on my skin and clothing was sometimes enough to set off bomb-sniffing machines.

I inhaled. The balance of my life was restored.

Faith's skin smelt of charcoal. A sulphurous odour remained in the room from those parts of her hair I had burned. J.D. Salinger, who helped liberate concentration camps in World War II, told his daughter, 'You never really get the smell of burning flesh out of your nose entirely. No matter how long you live.' Thankfully I had never experienced it on such a large scale.

"Just tell me what I want to know."

Her blue eyes turned to look at me but she didn't allow me the pleasure of knowing that she saw me.

"What good would it do?"

"The torture would stop."

"For me."

I shrugged. "Yes. For you."

When she sighed I could tell that it hurt her.

"You just don't *get it* do you?"

She was right, I didn't.

"Make it up. Everything becomes truth eventually."

She tried to sleep but I couldn't let her. She should have taken her chance whilst I was shopping.

We all should have taken the chance whilst we were shopping.

For some of us, all we ever did was shop.

Outer Spaces

Real life is what happens when you look away.

What do I remember? She's on all fours, a loose white t-shirt covering her upper body. Her head bent forwards, downwards in supplication. Her skin is pale, milky white, soft. Long black socks hug her legs up to her knees. The rest of her is exposed, inviting and waiting.

She's on the bed in a hotel room on the outskirts of my hometown. It's early evening and the sun is fading as fast as my memories. I get the fringes of another life somewhere but can't place it. I live in the moment and the moment is here.

Leaning forwards I run an extended forefinger along the back of her t-shirt, down her spine as far as it will go. She gasps. A shiver runs through her in the opposite direction. Her breathing quickens. I cup my palm around her mons and heat sinks into my skin. I insert a finger inside her, and like connecting a bulb to a socket, lights go on in my head, replay our encounter as I play with her.

*

16

I didn't have to go home that evening, at least not for a while. My daughter was with her mother and my wife was with hers, settling into familial roles like matryoshka dolls. A decidedly feminine concept. After work I'd joined Darryn and Simon in the pub. They'd been suggesting it for weeks, making jokes about being tied to apron strings. Truth was, I'd done the tying myself and wasn't going to make excuses for it. But I went with them because I knew I wouldn't hear the end of it.

They drank lager; I drank bitter. They talked about football; my mind wandered to netball. A crowd of giggling girls all wearing pink Stetsons and name tags barged into the bar and then out again, caught within a badly organised hen night. One of them looked over. I looked away. When I lifted my head up, Darryn and Simon were gone and my drink was still full.

Something shook the bar. Glasses rattled. Floorboard slats raised then fell. Staff became as attentive as meerkats.

Then it stopped.

And when I looked again, she was there. As though she'd turned sideways and slipped through a crack.

"Buy me a drink?"

She was younger. Was she too young? Was she *so* young that I shouldn't get her that drink, legally or morally? She knocked back a vodka so cleanly its taste must have been as clear as its colour, its smell. Her arm lay against the oak wood of the bar, skin the shade of balsa. Her fingers moved back- and forwards, not tapping but caressing a rhythm. Those fingers slipped into mine as we left the pub; gripped onto mine as I barged my way inside her; clung onto mine in a post-coital

17

embrace.

*

Routine bled her out of me.

Wake up. Get breakfast. Drop my daughter at school. Go to work. Go home. Eat. Watch TV. Go to bed.

*

We always shopped in ASDA on a Sunday. My wife bustling through the store, reading labels in close-up, eyes out for a bargain. Gripping the trolley I thought of those fingers. Imagined another life where Sunday mornings were nothing but bed. My daughter ran ahead, picked up some Coco-Pops and was told to put them back. Detritus of past lives clung to me in memory, actuality. She turned and smiled at me, and despite the pressing reality that childhood was forever slipping away there was still an innocence that pained me.

The store was heaving, filled with people that I wished I never had to meet. Forever searching for bargains we banged our trolley down aisles cramped with bodies.

Would she shop here?

I looked for her in the crowd. Wondered what would happen if I saw her. Wondered what would happen if she saw me. My wife's hand touched the small of my back, gently eased me along. Innocence.

For two nights spread across two weeks I had made excuses. Drinking with Simon and Darryn in the pub. If it was

18

questioned then it wasn't verbal. Each time I downed two pints in silence, sitting on a stool with my back to the bar looking at the doorway.

I made love to my wife disconsolately, with a dissociation that seemed to arouse her. I wondered what was going through her head. Through both of their heads. I wondered what was going through mine.

When I did happen to see her it was as though she had never been away. She linked her arm through mine as we walked over the river, using a pedestrian bridge that I couldn't remember seeing before. Booking us into the hotel we took our clothes off slowly, eyes fixed on eyes rather than bodies, trapped in each other's gaze.

She murmured as I touched her, fingers tracing a path around her curves, lips millimetres away as our tongues reached for a kiss. When she smiled, something turned inside me, the intimation that there was more here than I'd allowed. My lips moved down her body, over her navel, further.

When she came I saw a glass of water edging across the bedside table. The LED display on the radio alarm clock blinked off.

*

We never made arrangements but sometimes she would be there and sometimes she wouldn't. Reality unfurled when I was with her; strips of myself peeled away: identity, responsibility, memory. Sometimes there were overlaps, however distinct and separate I tried to keep things. A kiss. A touch. A word. We didn't use names. Too dangerous. She knew my situation. I was less sure about hers.

When I collected my daughter from school I saw her everywhere. In the faces of young mums, teachers, pedestrians. Always waiting for that nod, touch, notification of her presence. Always ready. When my daughter linked her hand in mine I almost pulled away. Too small, always growing.

I wondered what we do when we make choices. Do we create other selves? Switch the points on the railway track and ghost along other lines? At some point do we converge? Are phantoms the remnants of identity that can't make their way back?

My head split in two. Double life. One time an evening pulled into a weekend yet when I returned there was no intimation that I had ever been away. I wasn't sure if I was caught up in the moment or if magic were at play. In my garage workshop something had been completed in my absence. I pushed it to the back of my mind, into the outer spaces of my consciousness. Forgetting anomalies came easy to me then.

But after a while it started to blur.

*

We knew it wasn't just sex, but neither of us had the courage to voice it. At the crossover life melded together. *I love you.* I would see her in the supermarket as a transparent being, her hand in mine as my wife's hand in mine. Co-existing simultaneously, one superimposed over the other. Double exposure. I imagined living with her, how it would be, and as I did so she did. Her clothes hung in the wardrobe alongside my wife's; she lounged on the sofa within my wife; when I fucked her I never knew exactly *where* she was yet I knew *exactly* where she was. Little tremors ran though me, moments of truth. She took me to the fringes of imagination where perfection exists, but where it *only* exists. I knew it was her. And I knew why.

Routine bled her into me.

Wake up. Get breakfast. Drop my daughter at school. Go to work. Go home. Eat. Watch TV. Go to bed.

Each conscious thought, she was with me. Each moment to share, she was with me.

I looked at my face in the mirror and tried to catch myself out. I twisted sharply to one side, expecting for a slivered moment to see a surprised face static like a visual echo, but either I wasn't quick enough or it was too quick. My edges were sharp, features the same. Yet within me I knew there were two people. Two lives lived as one. Chameleon traces dependant on who I was touching.

If it was invasion of the bodysnatchers then she hadn't just snatched my body, but taken my soul and mind.

*

My partners developed a symbiotic relationship: two dissimilar organisms living together in close union. It was impossible to tell if they were aware of each other—although if there was knowledge it would be one way.

I gave up trying to understand it and just embraced it. I looked for reports on the TV, on the Internet, to see whether this had happened before. I was filling up with life. My perceptions became heightened. Leaves on the trees had sharper edges, their

21

colours more distinct. Voices were clearer, people seemed happier. Everything was snug, fitted together, as though the universe had resolved its differences and harmony had taken hold.

Objects moved around the house of their own accord. Some would be in two places at once. It became that it wasn't simply *her* and *she* that overlapped. Two worlds were created like bubbles merging and separating. I was the only constant.

My daughter said she had three mums. I didn't dare question her.

I still couldn't catch myself out in the mirror.

At some point, I knew, the illusion would burst. I would float away in the remaining bubble to a destination unknown.

And so I did.

Follow Me

Claire picked up her mark on the corner of Meredith and Silent Avenue. Without looking twice she crossed the road and entered the shopping mall. Glitzy window displays reflected her skinny frame, and she was almost lost within a sculpture of melted plastic tubing. It made her smile, but she was careful to keep focussed on the job. She wasn't paid to show anything other than bland emotion.

She rode the escalator twice. Nipping into HMV she could sense his eyes boring into the small of her back as she thumbed through some retro punk. She wondered what he looked like close-up, not having had time to examine him properly before the pick up. Not that it mattered. It was pin money, that was all. A little something to put towards the deposit on a new flat.

Leaving the shopping mall she felt her heart quicken. The route was down to her; she could take it anyway she wanted within the designated period, but she found it difficult to stay in the mall for much longer than twenty minutes. The faceless interior and equally unanimated people depressed her. She knew the risks, but unless they had been hushed up the agency's records were exemplary when it came to choosing their clients. To her knowledge, no one had ever been attacked.

Taking a left down Bagel Street she paused to stroke a calico cat warming itself on a brick wall in the sunshine. The cat's spine rose beneath her fingers, immersed within incredibly soft fur. She could feel the ridges under her touch, affirmation of a living being. If she listened hard enough she could almost hear his breathing against the background of soundtrack purr.

Traversing the High Street, dodging cars, she waited on the other side of the road for him to catch up. Feeling hungry she slipped into a Baker's Oven and bought a cream puff. Pausing at the door she heard his voice asking for a hot sausage roll, and she had to immerse her mouth in the cream to stifle a small laugh. Sitting on a round bench that surrounded a tree she ate the puff with her fingers, icing sugar dusting her prints. In the corner of her eye she saw him leaning against the side of the baker's. He'd done this before; she was sure of that. His eye contact was as tentative as hers. Their glances rarely met.

She checked her watch and found there were ten minutes to go. Getting up she threw her paper bag towards a cylindrical green bin, where it bounced against the lip before falling in. Walking down London Street she turned at the corner and slipped into another department store. She felt comfortable there. It was independent and contained less of the rubbish that she associated with the mall. His time ran out when she ascended the escalator, and upon reaching the toy section at the top she noticed he'd stopped following.

Crossing over to the elevator she hit the button for ground

24

floor and left the building. Another fifty quid in her pocket. By the end of the week she should have enough for the deposit.

Claire checked her watch. There was just time to make it across the city for her rehearsal. Weaving in and out of vehicles she crossed the carpark and made a dash for a yellow bus filling up with passengers. Slipping some coins into the driver's hand she pulled her ticket from the dispenser and sat down by the window.

It always took a few minutes to shake off the feeling of being followed, and she wondered how long it would take to develop a sense of paranoia. Not that she intended to keep in the job for ever. The band just needed a break, that was all. For the right person to see them at the right time, get a record deal, hit single, album, tour. That kind of thing.

She leant back in her seat, slipped the tiny headphones from her MP3 player into her ear. Drums beat around her mind as the world whipped past the window.

*

"You're late."

"Fuck I am not."

Claire pulled her bass out from the cupboard. Black paint peeled from its surface revealing orange underneath. She'd have to give it another coat sometime soon. Greg was fixing up one of the microphones, strumming his lead guitar with his other hand. Flannel kept tapping the cymbals, his foot permanently on the pedal of the bass drum. She didn't recognise the song, maybe he was trying something new.

Greg had shrugged at her denial, then ignored her. Twat.

She'd be happier if he was out of the band, but he was the first guitarist she'd met that wanted to play his instrument differently from everyone else. And that was exactly what she wanted from this band. A group that was prepared to be different, without associating difference as being the same as everyone else who strived to be different. He liked her songs too, saw something in them. And once she'd fought off his advances she couldn't deny that he put his heart and soul into playing them. Still, as a personality he sucked.

She pushed the jack into her bass and plugged herself into the amplifier. A tremor went up her arm but she ignored it. She began to pick out the strings, let the rhythm of the instrument take over. It hung low on her body, below her hip. She hated those bass players who tucked it up high, played with their arms in an L-shape. It did the instrument a disservice, somehow.

Flannel stopped playing and gave her a nod. "Any news?"

"Nothing yet. Still watching the post."

"How long has it been?"

Claire wondered if he was just making conversation. He must have known it was a couple of weeks since they'd sent off the demo. All of them held out hope, although the death of John Peel had certainly interfered with their plans.

"Thirteen days, you know that."

"Hey," Greg said. "Sounds like a great title for a song. 'Thirteen Days'."

"Sounds like a cliché to me."

"Have it your way," he muttered. Claire was sure that under his thoughts, if not under his breath, he had made some derisory comment.

"Look. Let's get playing shall we? We've only got this space for an hour."

The band shuffled into mode. When Greg hit the opening chords of 'Shall We Go There' the atmosphere in the room changed, became electrically charged. After the count of three, Flannel hit in with the drums, creating a cacophony of sound that Claire gradually began to weave her bass inside. Her vocals were half-shouted, half-sung over the top of the noise. She could hardly hear herself, but she knew it was good. She could tell from the playing of the others.

They played the same song another four times, then switched to 'Penny Black'. Claire screamed *philately will get you nowhere* over and over towards the end of the song. She watched Greg thrash his guitar as she did so, then abruptly change stance as his playing segued into the melodic outro that marked the end of the song. Flannel slowed his drumming down to a heartbeat. When the final chords faded they all knew they'd played it better than the demo.

"What next?"

"'Danger Man'?"

They ripped into it but Claire missed her cue at the start of the second verse, and Greg stopped playing whilst Flannel beat the same note repeatedly until the stares died down and they went into it again. Something was missing from the song, Claire knew that. 'Penny Black' was their standout, but 'Danger Man' was single material and they just couldn't get it right. She thought they'd had it right on the demo, but after the blistering performance of the earlier song she could no longer be sure. They finished the session with a couple more songs. Then left it at that.

Packing their stuff away Claire noticed her arms were exceptionally pale under the stage lights. Thin bluish veins ran vertically away from her palms. The corporeality of her body suddenly repulsed her, and she forced herself to look away. The others hadn't noticed, and she realised that Greg and Flannel were deep in discussion. When they saw her watching them they pulled away from each other, like schoolboys caught dissecting an insect.

"What is it?"

Flannel looked from her to Greg and back again.

"We were just wondering if you'd thought any more about changing the name of the band."

"We've had that discussion." She could detect a faint hint of desperation in her voice. "We agreed."

Greg stepped forward. "*You* agreed." He paused. Held his breath then let it out again. "Look, the songs are great, but Ultraviolent just doesn't do it for us. We need something a little more universal."

Claire looked at Flannel. "You agree with that?"

She saw it in his eyes before he looked away. He didn't, but he was going along with Greg.

She shook her head. "I don't want to discuss it right now. We've sent the demo off, we've got to wait to hear back. If you want to discuss changing names then why don't you change yours, *Greg?*"

"What's wrong with it?"

"It's hardly punk is it? Greg fucking Blackstock."

"Well Claire Plastic is a bit pseudo-retro, isn't it? Maybe I should become Danny Day-Glo or something. Jesus."

Flannel stepped between them. "Come on, break it up. Are

28

we going down the pub or what?"

"Not tonight." Claire continued packing away. "Next rehearsal is Thursday, right? We can do something then. I need to be alone this evening."

"You've got a date then," Greg muttered under his breath.

Claire pretended not to hear, but as she left the rehearsal space his voice echoed behind her: "You need me."

*

Her flat was too small. Too dismal. It might have suited the angst rock 'n' roll lifestyle, but even in the summer it was freezing and she never felt at home there. In winter it was bitter. True it was self-contained, there was no sharing of the communal kitchen that Flannel had to put up with in his digs. But in some way it also emphasised her loneliness.

She sighed and plugged in her computer. She wasn't sure whether bickering fuelled the band or destroyed it. Whether their internal anger assisted in combusting them on stage, metaphorically speaking. Whatever. She knew she didn't have sufficient talent to make it solo. Yet.

Her thin woollen cardigan failed to lower the goosebumps on her arms. Spring had yet to melt into summer, and the evenings remained too cool for her. As she typed her password into FollowMe.co.uk she could feel eddies of cold weaving in and out of her fingers. They felt brittle, devoid of substance. Abused.

Her account had already been credited with that day's earnings, and she double checked that it had gone into PayPal before transferring the total balance to her bank. A new message indicated that she had another client booked in for tomorrow, early afternoon. His face was the only information she had about him. Short, wiry hair, with the whisperings of a moustache. The image was black and white but she could tell his eyes were blue. There was a coldness about him too.

Mid-thirties? Probably. He was certainly older than her. She always got reassurance from that. It was the young that occasionally unnerved her, although she'd yet to refuse an assignment.

She logged out and checked her other emails. Then logged onto the band's website and updated her blog. On the outside, the pretence that something was happening made her believe the band was heading somewhere. But she dreaded those demos coming back in the mail.

She went into the kitchen and chucked a pre-cooked meal into the microwave. If she used the oven then at least she could warm her hands against it, but she was too hungry to wait longer than was necessary. When the machine beeped in readiness she removed the contents and sat cross-legged on the floor in front of the television. Channel hopping left little to the imagination.

By ten o'clock she was in bed. Her thin body curled tight for warmth. Surely it couldn't be as cold as this? Sigur Rós were on her CD player. Maybe they contributed to the cold.

She fell asleep convinced she was being watched.

*

She wasn't late, but he was already waiting for her on the corner of Meredith and Silent Avenue when she arrived. Crossing the road she entered the shopping mall. The weather had clouded over during her journey, and she valued the warmth of the mall over the possible rain-swept streets. He followed about twenty steps or so behind her. She was convinced that his shoes were squeaking although the concentration it took to hear the noise might have been sufficient to create the illusion in her mind.

She rode the escalator and entered HMV. Something was playing over the sound system that she neither recognised nor liked. Walking to the end of the alphabet she flicked through some U2 CDs. She wasn't a fan, but she imagined Ultraviolent alphabetical in the racks next to them. What was wrong with Greg? There was nothing exclusive in that name as far as she was concerned. It attracted just the kind of audience that she was looking for.

For a moment she forgot her mark, and then glanced up to find him watching her from the other side of the rack. He'd be in the *M*s, by her estimation. Not that he was looking for any music. His gaze remained fixed to hers until she found herself looking away.

Weird.

There was something about him that she found distasteful. Normally they liked to keep some distance, fulfil a fantasy. But his look indicated something extra at work. A desire for contact, but that certainly wasn't in her contract. When she looked up again, he was gone.

She glanced around the store, a little frantically. If she'd lost him that could mean a complaint and she wouldn't get paid. She needed that flat. A little warmth. Then she saw him again, standing by the exit. As she watched he raised his right arm to scratch just below his eye. The movement seemed robotic. Not quite right. There was something mechanical about the whole process.

31

She made her way over to the exit, intent on not looking his way. After a few shops were put between them she glanced into the great glass window that ran alongside Boots and saw to her relief that he was following her. Money in the bank.

Claire remained in the mall for the duration of the hour. The session ended as she drank dark bitter coffee out of a Styrofoam mug at a white plastic table. She could detect him behind her with the cappuccino she had heard him order. When she popped to the toilet she didn't expect to see him on her return. True to his payment, he had gone.

She ordered another coffee and forced it down, watching the shoppers go in and out of the stores. She wondered if there were any other followers working in the crowd, and if so whether she'd know how to spot them. It was a strange business but she couldn't argue against it. She even harboured that if Ultraviolent became successful she might count them amongst her fans.

There was nothing else to do that afternoon, and she was about to leave the coffee shop when she saw Flannel enter the mall in the direction of the escalator. Claire guessed he was heading to HMV. She smiled to herself and decided to follow him. To see how long she could do so before he noticed her. Getting up from the table she reached the bottom of the escalator just as he reached the top. She watched him turn right and then she began to ascend. Once her foot was on the metallic strips she found herself bound to her task. Carried along without control.

At the top she spotted him a couple of hundred yards ahead. The mall wasn't particularly busy. Office workers had returned to their jobs, and the mid-afternoon crowd was thinning out as mothers left to pick up children from school. If Flannel were

32

to turn around then he'd spot her easily, but that also meant it would be difficult to lose him. To her surprise he walked past the music store and ducked down a stairwell on the left. She wasn't even sure it held a public right of way. Then she realised it must lead to the carpark.

As she went through the doorway the building seemed to change, as though she were within some internal mechanism, slipping inside the flesh of the beast. Concrete steps led downwards, flanked by breezeblock walls. Footsteps echoed below her and then stopped. Claire rested against a metal banister and looked down the centre of the stairwell. Voices bounced up at her, the speech indistinct, distorted by the journey. She recognised Flannel's tones, and it seemed he was doing most of the talking. Then the sounds cut out and she heard footsteps ascending. Backtracking, she made her way to the doorway, then crossed the concourse and slipped into HMV. She decided to pick Flannel up when he reached the top, collar him for a coffee or something.

It took a while for the door to open, but when it did it wasn't Flannel who left the stairwell but her mark from that afternoon. As she watched he raised his arm to scratch a point below his left eye, and there was that same mechanical movement. Something turned inside her. She felt sick. Was that who Flannel was talking to, or was it a coincidence? Neither he nor Greg knew what she did for a living. Yet her image was on the website for those who paid for the privilege of seeing it.

She waited fifteen minutes, desultorily flicking through CDs in the rack. She didn't leave via the carpark. Didn't want the confrontation. Instead she headed for the main exit, and bought something from Tesco's for her evening meal. The bus ride home was filled with noisy youths. Suddenly she didn't want them to have any part of her music.

*

"Late again?"

"Fuck you!"

It was almost a mantra. Claire hefted her backpack onto the top of one of the amplifiers and gave Greg and Flannel a quick glance over. Nothing seemed to be different, but her allegiance to Flannel was slipping. She needed that to be constant, to be the anchor between her and Greg, just as the drums kept the two guitars in rhythm. But doubts congregated in her mind, clamoured for explanations.

She decided to hold her news back until later.

As she withdrew her bass from the locked cupboard her fingers received a blast of icy cold. The air-conditioning unit was temperamental at the best of times, but she had never felt it so strongly before. Looking across to Greg and Flannel she saw that they both wore t-shirts. Was it only her, or was the summer a long while coming?

"What are we starting with?"

"'Penny Black'."

"But we always start with 'Shall We Go There'."

Claire snapped. "This isn't a gig. It's a rehearsal. I want to start with something we're familiar with. Get us warmed up."

Flannel nodded, then turned his head away. She hadn't seen a touch of defiance in him before, but was that her imagination. When they played the song he seemed focussed

34

enough. So was Greg. They didn't need to play it a second time.

She got them to play 'Danger Man' next, but there was still an element missing. Maybe they needed some keyboards to round the sound out, although she wouldn't admit it. Greg had wanted to bring in a keyboardist awhile back—a guy from a band he had previously worked with—but Claire was having none of it. She didn't want the power shift that would come with it. To be sidelined within her own band.

As they ran through 'Armadillo', she found her thoughts drifting to those songs that Greg had written, that she knew at some point—come second album maybe—would start to work their way into their set. They weren't bad, she gave him that. But they weren't hers either. Too upbeat. Too summery. Despite her love of the heat, her songs were winter at heart. Colder sometimes than even she intended them to be.

As they ran through the middle eight in 'Armadillo', Claire suddenly spotted movement in the darkness in front of them. An angular, jerky motion. Around head height. She immediately stopped playing.

"Very fucking funny."

Greg and Flannel looked at her oddly.

"What?"

"Your friend, Flannel. Standing there in the darkness. Bring him along to freak me out, did you?"

"I don't know what you're talking about."

"The one you met in the mall. In the carpark. Don't think I didn't see you. Come on, get him out, get him up on stage."

Then the lights went on and Claire saw that Greg had flicked the main switch. The auditorium before them was empty.

He must have left the building during her accusations.

But the cards were in their hands now, she saw that.

"Scared of the dark are we?" Greg was grinning. "Are we going to continue playing or what?"

Claire sucked in her breath. Nodded.

"Hey." Flannel stood up. "I want to know what's going on. What's this all about?"

"Plastic got spooked." Greg was still grinning. "Stage fright."

"It's more than that. What were you accusing me of?"

Claire shook her head. "Nothing. That's all. Let's just get on with it, okay?"

Greg strummed a few chords out of his guitar. "Play one of mine for a change?"

"We're playing 'Armadillo'. We haven't finished it."

They played the song three more times before switching styles and finally ending with 'Contrariness'. They hadn't played any of Greg's songs at all, Claire had made sure of that. Today was her moment, and neither Flannel nor Greg were going to spoil it. If the crunch came to the crunch she could use session musicians anyway.

She'd been planning to tell them about it during the rehearsal, but the figure in the shadows had upset her scheme. As they packed their stuff away she suggested going to the pub, and Greg and Flannel readily agreed. She thought she caught a look between them as they did so, but there might have been nothing in it.

As they left the building she wondered whether she'd seen anything at all.

The Crown was half-full and they had no trouble getting to

the bar and then getting a table. Their personalities were represented by the alcohol they drank. Flannel was on cider, Greg on lager, and Claire had a pint of Adnams. As they took the liquid into their mouths and talked over the evening Claire realised that despite their differences they were in fact a tight unit. On occasions they could even be friends.

"Listen," she said, reaching into her backpack, "I've got something to show you." She rummaged around and pulled out a letter from the BBC. "They want us to do a session on the Mark Radcliffe show. A spot on unknown bands. Two songs. They've suggested 'Penny Black' and one other. What do you think? I reckon we should do 'Danger Man'." She smiled at their reactions. Everything was coming together.

Then it hit a dull spot.

"Radcliffe's Radio Two isn't he?"

That was Greg.

"What of it? It's not 1970 you know."

"I think we should drop 'Danger Man'. Or get some keyboards in. It'll sound flat as fuck in a proper studio."

"How about 'Double Negative Creep'? Your Radiohead/Nirvana homage?"

That was Greg's song. Claire couldn't believe Flannel had suggested it. "That's virtually karaoke. Give me a break."

"It's a good song, Claire." Flannel was calm. Looked her in the eyes. "This could be our chance."

"'Danger Man' could be a single."

Greg: "With keyboards."

Claire: "This isn't about you, you know."

Greg: "Why shouldn't it be? I'm just a part of this as you

37

are."

Claire: "This is my band. Has been right from the start."
Flannel: "Our band. Yours and mine. At the very least."
Claire: "My songs though."
Greg: "*Nice.*"

The beer swam around in Claire's stomach, as if it suddenly had a mind of its own. She could feel the acidic taste of bile rise in the back of her throat. Without saying anything she got up and made her way across to the toilet. Even before the doors closed she could hear Greg and Flannel talking about her. The comradeship of their manhood. Bolstering each other's egos.

Her fingers gripped the ceramic surface of the sink, but once she was in position the need to vomit left her. She spat twice, but nothing else came. Looking up into the mirror above the basin she was aghast at how pale she looked, almost transparent although she put that down to the fluorescent lighting. She needed to get a good meal inside her. Take a few days to think things over. If she wasn't careful, everything would implode before it began.

When she went back into the bar Greg and Flannel had their heads together. For a second they could have been kissing, but it was just whispered conversation. As they saw her and pulled away she thought a shadow remained between them. The residue of herself or the trace of someone else?

"Look, I'm going to get the last bus home. We can talk about this later, okay? We've got a few weeks before we have to make any decisions, but let's not do this for us. Let's do it for the band."

She left as they nodded in approval, but she knew the conversation would continue in her absence. How long would it be before they were playing with keyboards? Before they started playing more of Greg's songs than hers? No doubt they'd get a better bass player too, leave her as a figurehead on vocals. Well, she wouldn't play pretty just for them.

The streets were wet. It must have rained whilst they were inside the pub. Her trainers kicked shallow puddles as she walked, the street lighting streaking through the darkness as though slowly strained through gauze. She pushed her fingers deep into her trouser pockets, cursed herself for not wearing a jacket. She knew she couldn't stand the cold, so why did she insist on wearing that stupid jumper? She had half a mind to take it off and throw it over a wall into someone's garden. Force herself to take better care of herself.

She hadn't been well of late. Needed to get a better flat. Better heating. It was showing in her body, this lack of care. Her spiritual condition was making itself manifest in her physical appearance. She couldn't appear on stage like that.

It was all about connections: knowing the right people, being with the right people, having the ability to charm an audience, and having them desire to love you back. Yet it was also all about conditions: the audience conditioned to need the artist, the artist's need for acceptance. Maybe she had been swimming in circles too long, created a whirlpool and trapped herself within it, maybe she needed something outside of her music, outside of herself. The introspection which fuelled her lyrics might also be a barrier to success. Conditions. Connections. She just needed to connect.

Meanwhile, the rain started falling again in wisps.

Up ahead she saw a handful of people waiting for the bus,

and as it approached she quickened her step. On boarding she thought she glimpsed a figure sitting on the back seat, one hand over his eyes, but by the time she'd taken her ticket he was gone. She looked outside the window, at the lights from the bus strobing the pavement, reflecting in hidden puddles.

As they turned the corner she saw the man again. The one who had paid to follow her. He was standing watching her, without any hesitation. When he raised his arm to scratch his face she realised that it wasn't what he was doing at all. He had waved.

Just before he disappeared from view Claire lifted her own hand up. Waved back.

The Onion Code

I remember when I first deciphered a mobile phone message without seeing it, because it was around the same time that I'd discovered I could read onions. The police were less impressed with that latter ability, and only marginally interested by the former. I was forcibly ejected from Bethel Street police station until the events I had foretold became true, and then they sought me out in my Riverside apartment in the early hours following the quake.

I had been sleeping in my Hello Kitty underwear that my friend Kimi had sent over from Tokyo, but had the presence of mind to pull on my robe before answering the door. The earthquake similarities weren't lost on me, but the officers never discovered *that* connection. They entered an apartment that stank of onions. In my kitchen lay a dozen or so dissected segments, spread along the work surface in ever decreasing circles. Quartered onions lay in the four far-flung corners of the apartment, absorbing negativity and evil. Having slept through the quake that had devastated much of the city, I was convinced that my protections had been successful.

The earthquake had occurred at 2am, sneaking into the city under the cover of darkness. The immense structure of the Forum was the first building to succumb, large panes of glass dislodging from the ceiling and falling to the ground, smashing like sheets of ice. Nearby, the church of St Peter Mancroft only lost a few gargoyles, but the recently revamped Market collapsed under the weight of its newness, and the pedestriansed Gentleman's Walk buckled like dry snakeskin, pavement slabs rising as if the revealed scales of an underground beast.

As the sleep fell from my head like the flints off the Guildhall I became aware of the sirens and the panic and the non-nightly noise. But it was the insistent knocking that had wakened me and all the other sounds only pulled in around me after I opened the door.

"We'd like to ask you some questions," the first officer said.

"Here, if you don't mind," said the second. "Our police station is no longer there."

I nodded and asked whether I could make some coffee. They let me, and I watched the steam spiral out of the kettle as I pulled my robe tighter around me. As I bit back onion tears. As I remembered the events which had led up to this moment.

*

I had cut the onion on a Sunday evening only three weeks previously. Something in the way it fell caused me to notice it had split into perfect halves. The mince was already browning in the saucepan and I was late in preparing the spaghetti for my date: a newbie on the skateboarding circuit who I was quietly desperate to impress. But when the onion revealed itself my eyes were hypnotised by its concentric circles. Psychologically, I found myself pulled inside.

When I came out I was certain about the earthquake.

Subsequent research has led me to understand that I wasn't alone in finding the onion to be a particularly significant vegetable. The ancient Egyptians considered it an object of worship. Eternity was symbolically embodied in its circle-within-a-circle structure. Paintings of onions graced the walls of Egyptian tombs, and King Ramses was mummified with onions in his eye sockets. Of all the vegetables that had their images created from precious metals by Egyptian artists, only the onion had the honour of being represented in gold.

I turned off my mince and telephoned the police station.

"Hello? Listen, I know that this is going to sound crazy but an earthquake is coming. We need to prepare the city against the imminent disaster."

They took my name and address and said that they'd get back to me.

The next day, after receiving no follow up call, I tried again.

Then again.

And again.

Until finally I was threatened with wasting police time and I understood that my efforts would prove useless. Instead I spent hours examining onions to see if I might unlock the exact date and time of the quake. But this was as unsuccessful as impressing my potential new boyfriend had been—half-cooked mince not being his idea of a romantic meal.

43

"So what is this then?"

"Sorry, I got distracted."

He smiled. But not for long.

"An earthquake you say."

"I saw it in the onion."

"Yeh, well. I just remembered I gotta be elsewhere."

"See you around?"

"See you around."

I didn't see him around.

*

"You live here alone?"

The two policemen had fallen into the usual camps. One friendly and the other abrasive. I wondered whether they went on bad cop/good cop courses.

"Yes, I live here alone."

"No boyfriend?"

That was good cop. With a wink.

"Not at the moment, no."

"Tell us more about the onion."

"I thought I was wasting your time."

"That was then and this is now. Tell us more about the onion."

I didn't have much more to tell them. I cut an onion. I had a vision. I hadn't had any more visions.

"How bad is it out there?"

"Bloody awful." Good cop again. He received a glare from bad cop.

"Now, tell us about the mobile phone."

*

I had been exhausted. Two weeks after my onion discovery and all further attempts to probe the mystery had met with little more than sore eyes. I had emailed my friend, Kimi, in Tokyo but she had no answers for me either, although she hadn't been as dismissive as everyone else. I guess that the Japanese are a nation of eccentrics after all. But then weren't the English also supposed to be? Obviously Norfolk was a little straighter than everywhere else, which probably had something to do with the formidably flat landscape.

I shouldn't be biased. I was born here. In the old hospital which lay in ruins way before the earthquake struck. The new hospital was sufficiently far away from the city centre to avoid the catastrophe and therefore was actually of some use when it all came tumbling down. At last the location criticisms died away.

I was christened Maisie Annalise Winter in the church of St John De Sepulchre at the corner of Ber Street and Finkelgate. Not that I ever grew up to be religious. Both my parents died in a car crash when I was sixteen along the Acle straight. They met a vegetable truck heading the other way—although it contained beet, not onions. I guess it isn't often that life imitates the movies.

At twenty-three I finished my often-interrupted degree at the Norwich School of Art and couldn't find anywhere to put it to use. At the time of the onion experience I was working in a small fashion shop on Pottergate. It was in one of the changing rooms that I encountered the man with the mobile phone, and the second

45

phase of my recently discovered abilities began.

I had gone in there with a pair of Baby Phat Jeans and a FUBU top. The shop was quiet and as there were three of us working that day, we were taking it in turns to try out clothes. I was down to my underwear when the curtains swished in the adjacent cubicle and the small wooden bench creaked as someone sat down. *Trousers, skirt or shoes* I had thought. You wouldn't need to sit down for anything else. Then came the tap tap tapping of the mobile phone.

The keys on the mobile are universally placed, of course, and other than using it on a daily basis I'd never thought of their patterns before. Yet as he—I was later to discover that he was male—began to formulate his text I realised that I could decipher the message from the positioning of those keys. The small beep as they were hit was as effective as Morse code, and suddenly I had as much control over my senses as my entrance into the onion.

Four quick taps without pause. An *S*. Or possibly a *Z*. Two short taps after a slight vertical movement of the hands. Well, that had to be an *H* because an *N* made no sense. Diagonally now, and another two quick taps. An *E*. Then an apostrophe. Then another *S*. And so it went on as I quietly froze with fear.

She's in the next cubicle. I can hear her heartbeat. I can smell the onions.

I was torn between leaving the cubicle and remaining inside. My nerves were both heightened and shot to pieces simultaneously. It seemed like minutes before my legs could function after he left the cubicle. When I re-entered the sales area I was so disorientated that I was still in my underwear.

"Maisie! What are you doing?!"

I blushed and went back inside, dressing like a bewildered Mr Benn.

"Did you see someone go into the changer next to me?"

Beatrice and Alice exchanged glances.

"How could we not? He was kinda cute."

"He was male then?"

"Most men are!"

They giggled.

"Did you recognise him? Did he buy anything?"

But they didn't and he hadn't. Apart from his designer stubble, cool appearance, and winning smile they had no other factors to identify him. And I was under no doubts that I shouldn't tell them what I had *heard*. Instead I made an excuse to go to the bathroom and rubbed my hands vigorously with Cif lemon sparkle. Sniffing the air around me I re-entered the shop but could smell no more onion than I could when I first came to work.

I cut another that evening.

It told me nothing.

*

"And you're sure you were being followed?"

Good cop again. Bad cop was looking out of the window shaking his head in disbelief. He'd already sent a text on his mobile phone: *thank god ur ok*; so I knew his concern was no longer personal. I wanted to look out of the window myself. To see what damage had been caused. I wondered if I would make the papers. I didn't think that I wanted to.

"No, not being followed. Being watched. I was sure that I

was being watched."

"How could you know?"

"I've told you about the phone message. What other proof do you need?"

He shrugged. I got the feeling that this evening was too much for them. They probably weren't even sure why they were here.

And I wasn't sure how much that I could tell them.

After I had left work that day I walked up to Chapelfield Gardens and sat in the glow of the waning sun. Across the way a few skateboarders had fixed up a ramp leading from the bandstand but I didn't have my board with me and I certainly didn't feel like joining in. They were too young for a start, and for the first time ever I wondered if I were too old. I ran a hand through my thick dyed-red hair. I fingered my nose stud and studied my tattoos—at least, the ones I could see without being obscene.

I remembered my parents.

We argued often. Over what I could and couldn't do. Over what I should and shouldn't eat. Over who I could and shouldn't see.

When they died it was a relief.

And then the tears came.

*

In the week that followed the mobile phone incident up to the day of the eventual quake I signed myself off sick from work and travelled the Norfolk coast.

The air was clear and dry. The sunlight was fantastic. Grey-

48

brown sea morphed into the pale blue horizon and I captured it on canvas. Whilst I was painting, the Cromer lifeboat entered my vision and enacted a sea rescue for training purposes; almost for my benefit it seemed. I felt like waving. I thought of all the souls lost at sea. I felt like crying.

When the tsunami hit South-East Asia the previous Christmas, life had been reduced to numbers. I became drawn to statistics. I researched what I could. 150,000 people were estimated dead from the waves, yet the same year 500,000 deaths were registered in England and Wales alone. I wondered which figures were the most shocking. But then in 1998 only two deaths had really mattered.

When the lifeboat departed the scene, an object came out of the sea. A silver fish that shot into the air, twisted, buckled, then fell at my feet. I picked it up.

*

I couldn't tell them. They were disinterested anyway. Whatever might have been the truth I was just some crazy mixed up girl who had prophesied nonsense that had come true. There was no question that I could have caused the earthquake, there were no accusations of that. They didn't know what to do with me.

Bad cop looked over to good cop.

"It's terrible out there."

We joined him at the window, pressed together as we watched the view. We could just about see the ruins of the Cathedral and the toppled tower of City Hall. The latter building had been a monstrosity, but its destruction still made me feel sad.

The castle had slipped from its mound like a crown askance.

It all looked like a metaphor. I wondered if there were others who had been approached to hear their messages, for surely that was what had happened to me. Were there really no better ways to communicate?

*

The fish was made of solid metal. It was cool to the touch and surprisingly dry. The eyes were a deep green, a seaweed green. As I watched specks of red began to appear like tiny pupils. I picked the fish up and held it between the thumb and forefinger of my right hand. As I pressed the eyes the body split open into equal halves. One contained the future and the other contained the past.

I knew the truth. Or at least, that was how it seemed to me.

Like a *Mission Impossible* message the fish disintegrated shortly afterwards.

I sat on the bus to Sheringham with my painting under my arm. Nearby a young girl was returning from school. She held a mobile phone in her hand. *c u 2nite x.*

I thought she looked too young.

I placed the painting under the doorknob of my guesthouse room so that it couldn't be opened from the outside. Then I sat by the window. The salty breeze frizzled my hair. There were lights in the sea and lights in the sky. I felt distanced. Distracted. I didn't care about the *why me* anymore. I wanted to see my parents again.

There are signs for us everywhere. In the earth in the stars in the soil in the birds in the plants in the times in the receipts in the coffee in the tea in the leaves in the great plains of the Serengeti

50

in the silence in the light in the catacombs in the postcards in the oxygen in the tax office in the music in the heavenly bodies in the stratosphere in the very spheres in the phones in the fish in the onions. Everywhere. There are signs for us everywhere.

Our daily lives are close encounters of the third kind.

*

Good cop: "Churches will be full tomorrow."
Bad cop: "Fat lot of good that'll do."
Good cop: "They're gonna need it."
Bad cop: "Without understanding why."
Good cop: "It's better than nothing when it's all that you've got."
Maisie Annalise Winter: "Hey guys, come over here."

*

They followed me across to the kitchen counter. I had slipped away from the window and taken a look at the onions I had been slicing the previous evening. I felt something special was about to happen, and we watched as they started to move of their own accord. Their spirals spun like Catherine wheels, within the outer leaves of the onion itself, and so fast that the centrifugal force squeezed the juice out of them, spattering our faces and clothing. Somewhere inside there was a message. I didn't think any of us would be able to understand it, but suddenly bad cop stood bolt upright and scratched his head.

"Well bugger me."

51

*

I've since realised that their messages can only ever be effective when they're personal. Anything on a larger scale is simply too destructive. So we get fed little segments here and there, but the significance gets reduced to manageable concepts: *coincidence, deja-vu, serendipity*. I wonder how frustrated they must become to occasionally split from the rules. Cause an earthquake, a tsunami, an erupting volcano. A beet truck to slip across to the wrong side of the road. How much energy must be sucked from them to reduce people to numbers. To something we can universally understand.

When the cops had gone I emailed my friend in Tokyo.

Guess what. We've just had an earthquake!

It didn't take long to get a reply.

Congratulations. Join the club! We've just had a plague of locusts!

I knew she wasn't serious. Kimi was always like that. Yet, something stirred within me and I wondered if the earth was ready for extraterrestrials. Something actually in control of the world much more than we purported to be.

I knew I wasn't.

So later I sank my teeth into one of the raw onions, chewed and swallowed it down. I switched on the food blender and drank the juice that had a sharp semolina texture. I then stripped and rubbed a raw onion over my body, like an ancient Greek preparing for the Olympic games. The fumes rose and my eyes welled with tears, but like a crocodile's they weren't real.

I wore onion juice lipstick. Puckered my lips for the possible apocalypse.

Then I went out into the streets with my skateboard under my arm and wondered if there was anything I could do.

The Cruekus Effect

When she said *cruekus*, it all fell apart. We couldn't have known, but that simple mispronunciation led us down a road that hadn't prior existed. We slipped headlong into another reality, one that didn't know we were there and where we didn't belong. It took us a year to realise what had happened. And by that time, of course, it was too late to go back.

Mandy was three years older than me. A social worker in her mid-thirties. I'd only just turned that way, and was still finding myself, wondering when life was supposed to begin. Mandy had suggested that it was hitting thirty rather than forty, contrary to the popular saying, but that was only because she thought she'd turned herself around. And her saying that made me feel good, because I knew I was part of that. Part of her new life.

She told me she'd turned to social work because of experiences she'd had in her past. I never questioned her about them, the fact that they had such an effect suggested that they were well left alone. Anyway, I wasn't interested in her work, I was never one for caring. So long as she was happy and content that was enough for me, I didn't need the specifics. Although I did like hearing her say how much she loved me.

"My love for you would melt all the tigers in the world."

"You've nicked that from Murakami."

"Have I now?"

"You know you have. *Norwegian Wood*. Come up with something else."

"My love for you would freeze all the bears in India."

"Hmmmm . . . that'll do."

When I first met Mandy I was working in a call centre, persuading mostly old women to buy lottery tickets to help charities. As far as I knew it was a legitimate organisation, and I had no qualms in signing people up for it. The way I saw it, even if it wasn't legit, the ticket purchasers still believed they were helping a good cause. They got the feel-good-factor, regardless of whether it was genuine or not.

It was Mandy who answered the phone on one of my random cold calls, automatically assigned by a computer. We later laughed that it could have been anyone who took that call. In my more secure moments I even suggested she would have dated whoever called her, but we both knew it was fate, kismet, however you wanted to describe it, that eventually led us into each others' arms. I mean, what were the chances of that happening? Next to none.

I liked the sound of her voice. She liked the sound of mine. We had a few jokes. She even bought a couple of tickets into the lottery. Said she was feeling lucky. So was I. When I took her details I saw that she only lived twenty miles away and we agreed to meet for a drink. My supervisor was listening into the call, but she didn't mind because I'd already made the sale. Sometimes I wonder whether she should have stopped me.

The pub was called the Dog and Bucket, and was midway between us. Mandy had raven-dark hair, a full figure, and a smile that would melt a tiger. She bought the first round of drinks, and I knew I would fall in love. Not that this was unusual for me. I usually fell in love first, and then took time falling out of it. Sometimes it felt that I lived my life, although not intentionally, in reverse.

I can't remember what we spoke about, but it was probably her work. She enjoyed it. I've yet to meet a social worker before or since who said the same thing. But she explained this was due to her background; that she felt like a phoenix rising from the ashes then turning to help her fellow man. All I did was sit there and wonder how long it would take to get into her knickers.

So we dated a few months, and then I moved into her place. I had nothing to lose. I let the job go. Found another working in a sandwich bar. There was a disparity between us in terms of the income I brought into the household, but she didn't mind. I think she enjoyed the fact that she was controlling the finances, and—by default—somehow controlling me.

Of course, I let her think that. And to some extent it was true.

So we continued our idyllic lifestyle until she said the *cruekus* word. I don't know why it lodged in my mind. After all, at the time it meant nothing; but I've since pulled back the threads and realised that was where it began. And after that came Mandee, and latterly Pool. But I'm getting ahead of myself—perhaps a first.

We lay in bed, playing a game we used to get to know each

56

other. Mandy would say something like *Cornflakes* or *Rice Krispies*, and we'd each state our preferences; sharing the reasons for our decisions. It was a go-to-sleep-game. Something out of nothing, but just because we were lying together in the warmth, our bodies touching and in some cases entwined, its sum total was more than it was worth. And there wasn't even much repetition. If we thought about it, the game could go on for ages.

I'd just said *Clangers* or *Pogles*, to which her answer was *Clangers*. We had a brief discussion of children's television, and even emitted a few whistles, before Mandy spoke again.

Tulip or Cruekus?

I fell about laughing. *Cruekus?* What the fuck was that? The word had caught in her mouth, stumbled as it fell out.

Crocus, idiot.

Of course I knew what she meant, but the mispronunciation tickled me, and kept on tickling me. I couldn't stop laughing. For a moment, she joined in. Then she stopped, scowled; then joined in again.

Yet somewhere, a lever was pulled and the track we were on diverged.

*

We started mispronouncing words deliberately. After the cruekus event I started referring to her as *Man*dee, with the emphasis on the elongated second syllable. My name, Paul, was a little harder to play with, but Mandee soon came up with *Pool*, which was intensely annoying and made her smile even more so because of that. Soon it was Mandee and Pool this, and Mandee and Pool that. Somewhere inside us we were rediscovering an inner child. There was a playfulness in our speech which translated itself into other aspects of our lives. Not that we'd been serious up to that point, simply that now we had a structure to our silliness. Mandee joked and suggested I went through a midlife crisis during the day and a second childhood each evening. It was true that when I was making sandwiches and wasn't with her that I was introspective and dull. I often daydreamed of girls and cars, too.

It wasn't long before we were specifically looking for words to mispronounce. For some reason, animals were our most popular. Pen*guine*. *Ga*rnu. Ba-*jar*. (Being penguin, gnu, and badger respectively). We inserted them into the conversation whenever we could. We dared each other to mispronounce words whilst we were at work, and would make lists and compare them during the evening.

Is that ham and moostard, sir?
So you're Mr Smith's main careaaarrr?
Would you like that in a bap or a bigotte?
I'd like to refer someone to social services who has old timer's *disease.*
And so it went.

And each time we diverged from the norm, so did everything else. Leaving us . . . behind? Sideways? Who knew? But leaving us all the same.

On our anniversary we decided to have a meal at the pub where we'd first met. Mandee was working around that area on the day, so we decided to travel separately. In some ways, this added to the enjoyment because it emulated that first meeting. I arrived earlier than intended and noticed a few changes had been made. For a start, the interior had been redecorated, and rather than the homely old-time pub atmosphere I was familiar with, the insides were bright and airy. Lots of green and brilliant red. Still, I ordered myself an orange juice and lemonade and sat in the sun out front waiting for Mandee.

Fifteen minutes after we had been due to meet my phone buzzed. I had a text.

Where are you?

I answered her: *I'm sitting out the front, waiting for you. Where are you?*

I'm sitting out front, waiting for you.

I looked around, but unless Mandee had transformed into an elderly gentlemen complete with pipe and dog she was nowhere to be seen.

I can't see you.

Well, I can't see you either. You sure you've got the right pub?

I looked up at the sign and saw it as clear as day. The Dog and Bucket. I was about to text her back when I looked at it again.

The Doog and Bucket.

I phoned her instead.

"Come on Pool, stop messing about, where are you?"

I found myself shrugging, struggling to find my words.

"I'm at the pub. I'm sure it's the right one, even though they've redecorated and changed the sign."

"Redecorated?"

"It's all greens and reds."

"Not here it isn't. Well, they've done it up; but it's orange and blue. Bloody awful."

We both paused, thought for a moment. Then Mandee said:

59

"What do you mean about the sign?"

"It says the *Doog* and Bucket, not the Dog and Bucket."

"C'mon Pool, this is no time for games. I'm getting hungry here."

"Seriously. You say you're sitting outside. Describe it to me."

I could hear her sighing at the other end of the phone. Then there was a pause. Then she described everything she could see. Right down to the man with the dog.

"Mandee," I asked, my voice uncertain. "Take a look at the pub sign."

I could tell from the silence that something was wrong.

"Mandee?"

"It says it's the Dog and *Barket*."

"You're kidding."

"Do I *sound* like I'm kidding?" Her voice rose several octaves.

I had to agree that she didn't.

We were both silent for a moment. Listening to each other's breathing, the only indication that either of us were there.

I looked around. To the side of the pub was the carpark, and beside it was a large oak tree. It fanned out like a giant piece of broccoli, the trunk sturdy in the earth with a bench in front of it. I described it to Mandee.

"Yes, I see it."

"Ok, well walk over there and sit on the bench. Tell me when you're there."

But she didn't need to tell me, because as I walked over the grass, passed a quacking duck, over the gravel driveway, and broke

60

a few twigs on the way to the bench I could hear Mandee's footsteps over the phone taking the same route as myself.

Just before I sat down I heard the bench creak. She had got there before me.

When I did sit down, I wasn't sure whether I was sitting on her or not.

"Don't hang up," she said. Her voice was quiet, and if it was childlike it was the voice of a child just woken from a nightmare.

I glanced at my phone and decided not to mention my battery was low.

"Okay, so we're both on the bench," I said. "Can you feel me?"

I thought I could determine a head being shaken, but whether it was through the phone or displacement of the air around me I couldn't tell. I also thought I heard sobbing.

"Mandee?"

She sniffed. "It's okay, I'm alright."

But we both knew she wasn't.

We both knew I wasn't either.

"Pool," she eventually said, "this can't be right can it? I mean, neither of us are really at the Dog and Bucket, we're both at different places."

"Different timelines, different realities?" I proffered, shaking my head as I did so.

"But how can this be?"

"It can't. Maybe we're both dreaming."

I then recalled various theories about parallel universes. About how each time we make a decision the world splits in two.

And keeps dividing and keeps dividing each new moment, each new decision. It was nonsense of course, but I wondered whether somewhere there existed a *me* who still worked in the call centre, who'd never spoken to Mandee? And was there somewhere a Mandee who never became a social worker? Who, whatever vice she'd had (drugs, alcohol, nymphomania) had never been able to kick it? Was even now out on the street somewhere, begging or whoring? And if so, which was the real me: the one here now, or the one someplace else?

It was just then that my battery ran out.

*

I did what anyone else would have done. I drove home with the intention of charging my phone.

Mandee was in the kitchen cutting vegetables when I got back.

"Sorry I couldn't make it," she said.

Then, when she saw the expression of shock on my face, "You did get my text?"

I mumbled a *yes*, explained I had a headache and went up to bed.

I'd already plugged in my phone and checked my messages (*Sorry, been held up at someone's house. Will meet you at home. I'll cook! x*), before Mandee came upstairs.

She sat on the bed.

"You okay, honey?"

I couldn't recall her ever having called me honey.

"I'm making your favourite. Ratatouille."

62

Was that my favourite?

"Thought we might get an early night to make up for this afternoon."

I found myself nodding just as I drifted into sleep.

I didn't eat that evening. I blamed it on the headache and Mandee was fine with it. I noticed that she still called me Pool and didn't object when I called her Mandee. When she slipped naked into bed her body felt the same. I checked for the mole at the base of her spine and it was still there. When I pushed myself inside her she also felt the same, her moans were the same, and when she came I found that I'd been doing the same things I usually did when I made her come. But for me, it was automatic. For her, I had the feeling there was a nanosecond delay, as though she had to check her responses each time she reacted with me. Not on a conscious level, but maybe a sub-atomic one. Whatever that meant.

We lay in bed afterwards, staring at the ceiling which had only just begun to darken in the late summer evening.

"Mars Bars or Snickers," she said.

"Snickers of course." I lay there in the silence. Then I said: "Clangers or Pogles?"

"Pogles, of course. Pogles Wood!" She laughed. "We've done that one before. It doesn't count. Choose another."

We played the game for another ten minutes as I wondered who it was I was lying naked in bed with.

*

I went back to the pub twice more. Once it was as it had been originally. The second time it was the *Doog* and Bucket. I thought of asking the owners about the name, but realised how tragic I would sound. I decided against visiting again in case I found the Dog and *Barket* and from there went back to our house and found Mandee with someone else.

Not that there was anything wrong with how things were. On the face of it we remained happy, but ultimately Mandee was different, and repeatedly and subtly seemed less Mandee-like each time she left and returned to the house. I acknowledge people change, that each new experience taints or enhances us in some way, but I became obsessed with knowing which parts of her had changed through normal congress and which were different because she had changed completely.

I ate less. Slept more. Mandee began to complain that I was different, less fun, more distant. We mispronounced less. All the enjoyment had been sucked from it. I stopped working.

I found myself asking her if she thought people changed, but she answered: 'No, over time you just find out more about them.'

There was little else I could cling onto.

And so it went on. Each time we made decisions our lives diverged, further and further away from each other's. Or at least, I believed it that way. The truth is, each of us are prepared to live with someone who doesn't quite match our ideal. We put up with idiosyncrasies and annoyances, and our perception of who we share our lives with shades rather than colours our reality. Sometimes, it's the build-up of these little things, divergences from what we want and what we have, which causes a relationship to end. And so it was with us. Whether she was Mandee or someone else.

But somewhere, of course, way before *cruekus*, Paul and

64

Mandy are still living together.
Occasionally, I wish I was there.

Bigger Than the Beetles

Naoko ran to show her sister what she had been handed outside the school gates. Atsuko was two years older and went to a different school a couple of streets away. Their mother watched them as they spoke excitedly: Naoko showing Atsuko what she had been holding in a clenched fist. Naoko had refused to show her mother, although promised to do so later, once Atsuko had seen it first.

The truth was that her mother already knew what was in Naoko's hand, because several of the other mothers had already told her. Each child, it seems, had been given one sometime during the day. It was a growing frog, a small toy which when placed in water would expand. Just as if it were growing in real life. Naoko's mother imagined it was part of a science experiment, even though each of the girls had denied that a teacher had given it to them. She put that down to the love of secrets.

She watched as the girls were joined by Atsuko's best friend, Michie. All crowded around Naoko's hand. The excitement soon left the older girls, and by the time Naoko's mother had caught up with her they were already walking ahead of them, swinging their bags in their hands and talking about older things.

Naoko looked up at her mother. Her small round eyes were almost black, such dark pupils.

"Do you want to see my frog?"

Her mother nodded. She held out her hand and watched as Naoko placed it in her palm. A clear plastic wrapper surrounded the figurine. *Growing Frog* was written on the cover, in both English and Japanese. She smiled in amusement.

"Naoko, where did you get this?"

"A man gave it to me."

"Where?"

"By the gate. Just before you came." She looked nervous and added quickly. "Others have them too."

Her mother handed her the frog back.

"It's okay," she said. "You can keep it."

Naoko half skipped the way home.

*

Naoko's father examined the frog closely. He was tired. The train had been fuller than usual. He had eaten at a *tachigui* before boarding and each time his stomach pressed into the shoulder bag of the man in front of him he had become increasingly aware that the food hadn't been of the best quality.

The frog was green, with a yellow slash along its belly.

"This is wonderful," he said.

Naoko could see he wasn't interested. She dealt him the killer card.

67

"It grows," she said.

"Grows?"

He looked at it again. It was soft to the touch, not made of plastic. He assumed it must be porous.

"And we put it into water?"

"Yes!" Naoko said excitedly. "Will you help me?"

Her father stood to his feet. Through the serving hatch he could see into the dining area where his wife was eating some ramen noodles. She had cooked enough for both of them and he regretted eating during the day. His stomach felt like it might explode at any moment. He wanted to lie down.

Naoko pulled at his shirt.

"Okay," he said. He led her into the small walled garden at the back of their apartment. They had been lucky to obtain this apartment, with its spacious living area and secluded garden. Even now, even when his stomach ached, he couldn't help but stop and appreciate what they had. In the distance, always in the distance, the sun was beginning to set and it cast a beautiful orange glow over everything. Over Naoko's upturned face, as she searched for a container within which she might place the frog.

Her father helped her. He located a red plastic bucket which they occasionally used when they took a trip to Kyujyukuri Beach. Returning inside the house to fill it with water he then came back outside and placed it near the door.

"Here," he said. "Put your frog in there."

Naoko looked at the bucket. Then she looked at the frog.

"It isn't very big," she said.

Her father laughed. He laughed so much his stomach began to hurt, and then he stopped laughing and patted Naoko affectionately on the head.

"Just how big do you expect the frog to grow?" he said.

*

Naoko could hear her sister breathing whilst she slept. They shared a bedroom even though there was space in the apartment for them to have separate rooms. When they first moved here Naoko hadn't wanted to sleep alone, and at only five years old her parents had granted her wish. Over time the other bedroom had come to be used as a playroom. Atsuko didn't mind, but Naoko knew it wouldn't be long before she would want a room of her own.

Naoko could hear her sister breathing and she wondered if she were dreaming about the frog. If Naoko had been asleep she was sure that *she* would be dreaming about the frog. But when Naoko finally slept she didn't dream about the frog at all.

Naoko's mother and father were talking about the frog.

"It doesn't take much to please Naoko," her mother said.

"Give it a day or two and she'll forget all about it. Then we can get rid of it," her father said.

"Why should we get rid of it?"

"Because the size that Naoko's expecting it to grow will mean that we won't have space for it," smiled her father.

"Perhaps we can put it in the spare room," said her mother.

Naoko's father laughed. He could laugh easily now. His stomach didn't hurt anymore.

When they turned off the lights he was well enough to play *hunt the frog*. Naoko's mother liked that game.

*

Early in the morning Naoko awoke. She couldn't remember her dream apart from the knowledge she hadn't dreamt about the frog. She wondered if that was an omen.

Atsuko was still asleep. Naoko slipped out of her nightclothes and pulled on her school clothes. Then she quietly opened the door and let herself out into the corridor. Atsuko opened an eye as the door closed. Then she fell back to sleep again.

Naoko fiddled with the lock on the rear door and managed to open it out into the garden. She looked at her frog. It had grown! Already the limbs of the frog were touching the sides of the bucket where only yesterday they hadn't. Naoko took the frog out of the bucket. It felt cold. Although it had been a warm evening the temperature must have dropped during the night. Naoko wanted to take her frog to school with her, but the man's instructions had been clear.

You must take this frog and keep it submerged—do you understand what that means?—in water for the next five days. Everyone has a frog, but everyone's frog is special.

Naoko placed the frog back into the bucket. She hoped that taking it out for several minutes wouldn't stop the frog from growing. She wanted to have the largest frog in her class.

*

During class, when the teacher wasn't looking, the children passed around drawings of what approximated to be the size of their frog. Naoko was convinced that some of the drawings were exaggerated.

70

She attempted to draw what she considered to be the exact dimensions of her frog but it was hard to do that from memory, and her frog must have grown during the day, so she made an allowance for that growth. Considering all the frog drawings it seemed her frog was of average size. She was happy that she had drawn a true picture of her frog. That she hadn't told any lies.

At morning break the teacher found all the drawings of the frogs and looked at them curiously. He knew they must have been drawn whilst his back was turned, and so just before the next lesson he made a great show of tearing them up and putting them in the wastebasket.

Naoko didn't mind. All she could think about was returning home that evening and looking at the size of her frog.

When her mother picked her up from school she didn't dare ask about the frog. She hoped her mother hadn't looked at it during the day. She wanted to be the first person to see the size of her frog, to see how much it had grown in her absence. As they walked passed Atsuko's school, and their mother waited for Atsuko to appear, Naoko shuffled her feet against the pavement. Michie, Atsuko's friend, came out first. Naoko liked Michie, but she hoped Michie wouldn't ask her about the frog. Yesterday her interest had passed quickly. Naoko didn't want Michie to be interested now. She didn't think the frog was meant for older children, or grownups. The frog was for children just like her.

Atsuko appeared. She didn't ask about the frog either. Unlike yesterday they dawdled behind Naoko and her mother on the way home. They didn't skip off in front of them. Naoko was glad. That meant it was almost guaranteed she would be the first to see her frog.

71

When they arrived home she ran through the house from front to back in seconds. When she saw the frog she couldn't believe her eyes. It was so large its head was out of the water, peeking over the top of the bucket. It must have doubled its size, she thought. She went back inside and pulled on her mother's arm. Naoko's mother came outside and looked at the frog with her.

She seemed to look at it for a very long time. And then she said, "I think we need a bigger bucket."

Naoko clapped her hands, delighted.

*

When Naoko's father returned from work he was holding a large plastic washing-up tub. Naoko's mother had telephoned him at his office and asked him to pick up a container on the way home. He had felt rather foolish, holding the tub on the commuter train, pressed up against the other passengers, even though the tub was wrapped in brown paper and no one could clearly see what it was. Not that it mattered. The train wasn't as busy as yesterday, and his stomach was completely better. Not only that, but several other passengers on the train were also clutching similar packages. He wondered what was inside their layers of brown paper.

Naoko's father filled up the plastic tub with water from the kitchen sink. It was heavy, and as he walked to the rear door he was careful not to spill a drop. His wife liked her floors clean. Sometimes he thought she spent all day cleaning the house, but in reality he imagined she spent most of her day watching television.

He tipped the large green frog from the small red bucket into the bright orange washing tub. Naoko watched him closely, as

72

if it were a real frog that might get hurt if he wasn't careful. But Naoko's father was more than careful.

Then he stood back and watched the frog. Like a flower you couldn't actually see it grow. You only knew it got bigger by comparing how it was to how it looked the last time you had seen it. He smiled at Naoko and patted her on the head. It had certainly grown larger than he imagined it might have done.

Stepping back from the tub he looked out over the small garden. The sun, once again, cast everything in a bright orange glow. Almost as orange as the bucket within which the frog now rested. And once again, Naoko's father felt blessed at the life which they led, with his two beautiful daughters and his loving, caring wife. Perhaps they would have a son one day. He had wanted a son from the beginning, but he would be happy with his daughters. His wife would take some convincing to have another child, but out here in the sunset none of that really mattered.

*

The next morning Naoko was first outside again. The frog had grown much larger overnight, and there were still almost four days to go within which the old man with the long grey moustache had told them to keep the frog under water. *Submerged.* Naoko realised she hadn't known the meaning of that word until the man had spoken it. Then everything was clear.

At school all the talk was of the frogs. Naoko didn't have one special friend, not like Atsuko had Michie, but she was a friend to everyone and everyone spoke to her about their frogs. There was a lot of talk about how big their frogs would be on the last day of

73

the week. The frogs had been handed to them on the Monday, so they decided that on Saturday—when there was no school—some of them would meet and have a frog measuring contest. The winner—the one with the largest frog—would get some sort of prize. No decision was made on what that prize would be, but it didn't really matter. What mattered the most was who would have the biggest frog.

*

During the course of the next three days Naoko felt that her father was turning against the frog. Thursday night, when he returned home from work, he hadn't bought the larger container that Naoko's mother had asked for. Naoko had cried and was sent to her room where her pillow became wet with tears. She was worried the growth of her frog would be stunted because already his limbs were pushed to the side of the container within which he now rested. She wanted to win the competition, but most of all she didn't want her frog to be the smallest. If she couldn't win, then she didn't want to be the greatest loser.

She wasn't allowed to look at her frog that evening. When Atsuko came to bed she was angry at Naoko for making her mother and father argue.

"It's the fault of your stupid frog," she said. Then she got into bed and pulled the covers over her head.

Naoko waited until Atsuko had fallen asleep and she could hear her breathing. Then she got out of bed, pulled on her dressing gown, and slowly opened the door of their bedroom. Quietly she walked down the corridor and stood outside her parents' room and

74

listened.

From inside the door, she could hear voices.

"It's unnatural. I've been speaking to some of the other men at work, and even on the train. These frogs are growing at an incredible rate. What if there's something sinister about them?"

Naoko couldn't hear her mother sigh, but in the space between her words she guessed it.

"The other mothers are saying the same thing, but what can we do about it? She lives for that frog."

"If it gets any bigger then it's going. That's my final word on the matter."

Naoko crept back along the corridor, passed her bedroom, and opened the rear door. In the light of the moon, with the frog's head poking over the top of the plastic swimming pool, it seemed to be looking straight at her.

"Don't worry froggy," Naoko said. "I won't let them take you away from me."

The frog said nothing but continued to grow.

*

On Friday morning all the classes were called into the main auditorium. Mrs Nakatani, the school principal, addressed them. Their mothers stood at the back of the hall.

"Children," she said; and the way she said it made everyone, including Naoko, a little anxious at what was to come. "Children, it has come to my attention that on Monday a man handed out *Growing Frogs* to each and every one of you. These frogs are nothing to do with the school. We have not authorised them.

75

We have reported the matter to the authorities and tomorrow morning a truck is coming to each of your homes to remove the frogs. From all reports they are getting too large to be of any use to anyone. In the meantime, please stay away from your frogs. And," again, that emphasis, "you are *not* to talk about them to anyone during school today."

The mothers filed out of the rear of the hall.

Several of the children, Naoko included, had tears in their eyes.

How can we keep the frogs? they thought. They whispered plans to each other during break times, but in their hearts they knew it was the end of the line for their frogs. The authorities had spoken.

When Naoko returned from school her mother let her take one last look at the frog. The frog was larger than her mother and her father put together, and totally filled the plastic pool in their garden, so much so that the sides bulged out as though they might split. Naoko's mother rested her arms on Naoko's shoulders, and gently kissed the top of her daughter's head.

Atsuko also stood in the garden. She was feeling a little jealous that she hadn't been handed a frog too. Michie was there as well. Michie didn't have a younger sister, but she knew why she and Atsuko hadn't been given frogs. They were too old to take the frogs seriously, and Naoko had been just the right age to take care of her frog properly. Michie thought it was the biggest frog she had ever seen.

When Naoko's father returned home from work he found his wife and two daughters and Atsuko's best friend, Michie, standing in their small garden looking at the giant frog. He was glad the frog would be leaving them soon. It was quite simply too big to be of any use at all. As he walked behind his wife, lightly placing a hand on her bottom, he heard a noise that started to vibrate the sky.

It began as a low hum. Then, as though the sunset had been speeded up on a DVD player, the sky turned black extraordinarily quickly and began to fluctuate, as if something were disturbing its very nature.

That something turned out to be the beating of black wings. As Naoko's father and his family watched, hundreds of gigantic beetles began to descend on the city. Their antennae flickered back and forth, as though they were seeking something specific. Naoko's father couldn't move. Even though he knew they were looking for humans. All of them were transfixed by the sight which had taken over the skyline. In the distance, he thought he could hear screaming.

Naoko knew what to do. She squirmed out of her mother's grasp and ran towards the frog. When she approached the head she gave it a quick tap. As the frog opened its eyes she told it that it was special. The frog gave her a private, personal, smile. Then it heaved itself up onto its hind legs, and directed its face towards the sky.

In other gardens, other children had been compelled to do the same.

One by one, giant tongues ascended into the sky, like pink fireworks shooting up with the precision of a pre-planned display, their sticky ends catching onto the beetles that flew over the city, pulling them back into the frogs' mouths where they were chewed and digested. Each frog must have taken down at least thirty beetles, until there were no more insects left in the sky. Naoko

77

couldn't keep count, but she was sure her frog had taken down the most beetles of all.

When the beetles were gone, and the sunset arrived as normal, an orange glow spread from the bottom of the garden, across the expanse of the giant bloated frog, and onto the faces of Naoko and her mother and father and sister and her sister's best friend, Michie. There was still a lot of warmth left in the sun, and each of them felt that warmth, and it was wonderful to be able to do so. To appreciate the feeling of being alive.

Saturday morning the trucks didn't come for the frogs. After another week they left of their own accord, suddenly, with no one seeing how or where they went. But Naoko knew that somewhere they were safe. Perhaps in the sea, or lying in the mud at the bottom of Lake Ashinoko. Just waiting there. Until someday they were needed again.

Pansy Blade Cassandra Moko

It starts with the desire to achieve more than her current existence. For her, this means it begins with boredom.

On the 12th November 2008, Pansy Blade lies on her back and holds her right arm aloft for a period of five minutes. After this time she becomes desensitised—her arm dissociating itself from her body. Without motion, it becomes something other.

She repeats the practice every hour until she is ready for more.

During the day she saves lives.

She wears a tight-fitting red Lycra suit. A gilded mask covers her eyes. Black knee-high boots complete the ensemble. An everyday girl in Superwoman's clothing. Whilst she can't leap buildings in a single bound, she can scale them faster than most of us. She takes some pride in rescuing an old couple from the crush of their crashed car. Remoulding the vehicle, reversing the crump. Firemen ask for her autograph. She shrugs.

What's a girl supposed to do?

Unlike the comic book hero she has no alter ego.

79

She can't do anything socially.

She wipes the minds of those she fucks.

Her costume is held together with a single zip that runs down the front. The top section comes apart easily, but she has to peel it away from her legs. A yellow strip hides the zip, resembling a go-faster stripe.

She has no memory of her past and no knowledge of her future.

On the 13th November 2008, Pansy Blade holds aloft her left arm. She stares at the ceiling. A single crack attempts to divide the room yet stops at mid-point, going nowhere. She anthropomorphosises the crack; gives it an identity it doesn't possess. She imagines its frustration at being unable to progress any further, unless acted upon by an external force. She wants an external force to act upon her.

After five minutes her arm no longer feels part of her body. It hangs suspended in the air, with as much identity as the crack. At that precise moment, Pansy Blade gains some relief from her individuality; becomes one with inanimate objects. When she wriggles her fingers, the illusion collapses. She realises it was no more than illusion.

*

In her suit she traverses the city. Liverpool is quiet. So many new buildings, so little to see.

She finds a small boy, lost, crying. She reunites him with his parents; fights the urge to lose the three of them. Why do we seek completion instead of confusion? This is what she is really fighting against: her desire to undo the world; to unravel rather than ravel; to create questions rather than answers. The father shakes her hand and she can feel the tension within him. Even though she cannot see into the future she knows the future here. He holds her hand for a second longer than he needs to.

From there she climbs the Liver building, overlooks the Mersey. This is her common seat of rest. She finds comfort knowing that the two birds which sit atop the building are looking in opposite directions: one to sea, one to shore. Local legend has it that the birds face away from each other, as if they were to mate and fly away the city would cease to exist. There are times when Pansy Blade wishes to face herself, to find out *what* would cease to exist.

On the 14th November 2008, Pansy Blade holds both arms aloft over her head. Without needing to concentrate they *appear* no longer connected to her, but she knows it is only an appearance. Ten minutes later she can't believe she can move them. So she tries it, does, and once again the moment passes.

She sighs. Rolls over onto her stomach. Slides a pre-cooked meal into the microwave and eats it out of the plastic tray after the beep.

There's nothing on television. There's rarely anything on television.

She holds out her arm after her meal, but the food in her stomach distracts her. She gets up, takes a bath, changes into her suit, conceals her nakedness. Searches for trouble because there is nothing else to do.

The City Records first mention Pansy Blade in '97. She has examined those records and the date holds little relevance. Her act of heroism prevented a rape. The man drowned in the Mersey. The female watched him fly through the air in awe. A simple jerk from Pansy Blade's hand and he was away. A legend was born.

Like an atom which suddenly appears from nowhere, Pansy can recall nothing other than this. She exists. She has purpose. She is so fucking bored.

From the top of the Liver Building she regards the city under cover of darkness. Lights populate her vision. From here they illuminate nothing other than themselves, constellations of star-like sparkles. Her suit keeps her snug. She feels neither cold nor heat. Neither frigidity nor passion. Sometimes she just needs to die.

People don't even point up at her any more.

She wants to use the extraordinary to improve the ordinary.

She sits there awhile, contemplating the city and everyday lives. Then she returns to her apartment, extends her hand again. When she senses that her arm no longer feels part of her body she closes her eyes. She imagines her soul. She imagines her soul floating through her chest and hovering over her body. She views it askance, detaches herself. Until her soul no longer feels part of her. Until it *is* no longer part of her.

*

She names herself Cassandra Moko. She has nothing to wear other than the clothes in Pansy's wardrobe. The suit isn't a good fit. She is curvier in this body, which surprises her because she thought she'd be intangible.

She runs from one end of the room to the other. Is out of

82

breath. She loves it.

She bounces on the bed. Creaking reminds her of fucking. She wonders whether she can have a proper romance, given time. Part of her wonders if she wants to.

She takes a bath. The water is sweet on her skin. She alternates the temperature from almost unbearably hot to certainly unbearably cold. She wants to feel those extremes.

"Hello."

She says the word aloud. Her voice is clear, doesn't waver. She has a conversation with herself which feels like a conversation with other people. Words tumble out of her. She laughs and the sound refreshes. She catches her smile in a mirror and it is real. The shock pulls her out of herself and when she wakes on the bed she is Pansy Blade again.

Emotions are brittle inside her. She opens her mouth but can't speak; has no one to speak to.

Holding her head in her hands her existence is heavy.

*

After a night without sleeping she goes shopping. She accumulates clothes easily; stores are only too eager to service Pansy Blade. She overhears speculation. It is well-known that her wardrobe is limited to red Lycra, latex, and PVC. She holds a dress up and has to wipe the memory of the shopgirl who serves her. She can't break the myth because it would taint Cassandra Moko. She is unsure how she chose that name.

Back in her apartment she places the packages on the bed. La Senza, Karen Millen, Oasis, USC. Doing her duty she rejoins the city. Alerts the police to a man dying at home, his angina spray inches from reach. Rescues the proverbial cat from a proverbial tree, the feline's nose pushing against her palm in wet relief. Prevents a minor drug deal out in Knowsley Park without wondering why she bothers.

Above her the hot sun strips males out of t-shirts, places women in short skirts, creates children with ice-cream running through their fingers. She doesn't quite see it.

Yet in her apartment. Naked. Her back on the bed, the clothes safely away, she closes her eyes and holds out her soul. Visualises everything displacing, shredding away. Once, when she slips into self-awareness, she falls backward and becomes Pansy again. She opens her eyes. Sees the crack. Closes them again and resumes the discard. Within twenty minutes she is Cassandra Moko.

She made good choices. The clothes fit. She pulls on French knickers, feels the silk against her own silky thighs. The bra cups perfectly. The dress is light, understated. It's mid afternoon and she decides to walk.

The heat hits her as she hits the street. Her room faces north whilst the sun's in the south, but even so the difference is palpable. She gets to enjoy her surroundings, gets to love her freedom. As she walks she can feel the passing of air, her senses heightened. She journeys down to the docks, slips into the Tate. In a sculpture room she regards John Davies' work, *The Redeemers*. The posture of the two men is suggestive, slightly sinister. Their hands imply menace, their closeness implies collusion. Their lack of hair, creepy. And the brown silk shawl worn by one of the men unnerves her. It appears natural yet alien simultaneously. It reminds

84

her of herself.

When she enters a bar no one looks at her. Without her mask she isn't remotely beautiful. Just an average girl with an average body doing average things. She sips a glass of wine, regards the street, wonders what would happen should trouble occur.

At that moment, reminded of her other self, she wakes on the bed and cries.

*

She becomes conscious of her voice. She sings in the shower. Buys music, books, art. What was once a bare room, a bed, a costume rail, the minimum of cosmetics, becomes a paean to existence. Before she was saving other people's lives now she is saving her own. As time progresses she spends fewer moments as Pansy Blade. Having shed that skin she wants to hide it. Secrete it.

She invites herself into the houses of others, and doesn't have to wipe their minds when she leaves. She creates friends through her own creation. Lies about her job, her seemingly limitless income. Lies about where she lives. Lies about her past, her parents. The more she integrates into society the more she finds she has to lie. Eventually, she *does* wipe their minds when she leaves.

"I like you when you sleep."

She gasps.

"I fell asleep?"

He nods.

She considers the possibilities.

"Can I call you Cassie?"

85

It is her turn to nod.

He nestles into her. She feels a closeness previously unknown to her.

Now when it's hot she wears an extra layer of clothes. When it's cold she removes them. She wants to feel those extremes, not to become used to anything. She understands everything can be snatched away at any time.

Occasionally, Cassandra can no longer recall her past. She sees newspaper cuttings about Pansy Blade and wonders whether she collects them. Other times, she sees the line retreating backwards, from herself to Pansy Blade to someone else who had once lain on their bed with their arm in the air. But she can't quite see the face of creation.

Surrounded by the new buildings of Liverpool One she eats a chilli chicken wrap bought at Pret a Manger. The taste peppers tiny explosions in her mouth. Sitting at the top of a series of stone steps she can spy an edge of the docks, the swell of the Mersey, the female of the Liver birds. She suddenly desires an overview of the city—not only from height, but from past present and future. She wants completeness.

She knows the Liver Building is reputed to be the Gothic inspiration for both the Manhattan Municipal Building in New York and the Seven Sisters in Moscow. She realises knowledge doesn't add completeness but makes her understand how impossible it is to be complete. Sometimes, even in this existence, she realises that the more she knows then the more she realises there is to know.

But if sometimes Cassandra forgets Pansy, Pansy *never* forgets Cassandra.

*

She peels on her Lycra skin, pushes her feet into her boots, arranges her mask with a quick glance in the mirror. Beside the bed yesterday's newspapers query her existence. She begins to query her own existence. Was she born from the collective imaginings of the city's population? Did their desire for a crime-free climate create her as their saviour? If they start to forget her, will she start to fade?

She knows she is raising more questions than there can be answers. There is ever only one answer.

But another question: if Pansy Blade ceases to exist would Cassandra Moko also cease to exist?

She knows the answer to that one.

She takes the hand of a blind man as he crosses a busy street in the knowledge that he will never realise it was her who had helped him.

There is anonymity and there is anonymity.

She wonders whether she could climb the Liver Building and have the strength to turn the birds to face each other, to see if the city would cease to exist.

Pansy has residual Cassandra memories. She seeks out her lover. Fucks him. Wipes him.

Afterwards she realises with a hollow laugh that she was jealous.

She is no longer bored. Considering she is only herself for ten per cent of the day she finds there is much to do. There is greater satisfaction when she helps the public. She no longer regards them with the disdain which had started to seep into her heart. Pansy reclaims herself as a superhero. People wave to her again. She sees smiles alight on their faces. Can sense the joy bursting out of them as they regard her with the knowledge that something is greater than they will ever know. She recognises the hope that brings. The possibility of something wondrous acquitting the surety of their deaths.

Pansy decides to be sociable.

She enters the bar where Cassandra regularly takes a glass of wine. The barman smiles, doesn't know he's already flirted. She orders a coke, doesn't want to trash her reputation. A group of young men shyly approach. She signs beer mats. They return louder than they came, one of them touched her costume when he thought she wasn't looking. A tremble of excitement rushed through her body faster than a speeding bullet.

She knows more than ever what it is to be alive.

In the evening she fights the urge to close her eyes, but through repetition alone habit dominates. When she rises as Cassandra she has no knowledge of her alter ego.

She wanted to use the extraordinary to improve the ordinary, but instead found she used the ordinary to improve the extraordinary.

She has no memory of this.

Cassandra chooses clothes for a summer evening. Wonders why she fell asleep in the afternoon, wonders why she often cannot recollect moments in her day. Is she narcoleptic? Should she see a doctor? She can't decide whether it would be a good or bad thing to find out.

At her lover's apartment he seems distant. They eat in a restaurant with a solid reputation, but the food tastes bland, without extremes in flavour. Background music is trite, spoils the atmosphere rather than improves it. When they share a kiss in his doorway she doesn't want to go inside. When he cites work as an excuse she sighs in relief. She knows it will be the last that she sees of him.

She walks back to her apartment. She wants to run but doesn't want to look stupid. She flinches when a group of males passes her; turns her head to one side when a gaggle of girls does the same. Her shoulders hunch inwards; there's a cool breeze in the air. When she looks up at the Liver Building she thinks she sees movement.

A bird stretches its wings. Looks from east to west and back again.

Another bird does the same.

On the ground, Cassandra shields her eyes against the dark. Searches for a flash of red. She has heard about Pansy Blade but has never seen her. She has read some of the newspaper cuttings that scatter her apartment, wonders about this obsession which she can never recall. She wonders what it would be like to be her.

The birds face each other. The city shimmers as if a mirage.

Cassandra shakes her head. Continues walking. Continues.

*

Pansy Blade scans the city from the top of the Liver Building. She sees a woman watching her from a distance. Is tempted to wave. Something about the woman attracts her attention. Possible suicide? She always finds those harder to avert. Everything kept inside.

Nevertheless she follows the woman, first with her gaze and then on foot. She watches her traverse the dock; attempt to locate her reflection within the black water. Does a circuit before heading residential. Looks from side to side before entering an apartment. Pansy scales the wall, her fingers dislodging fragments of brick onto the pavement. When she reaches a window she regards the woman as she undresses, showers, climbs onto the bed. She watches as she raises a hand in the air.

She knows her.

On the 6th August 2009, Apex Gale performs her first ever rescue. Afterwards, she wonders how she came into being. But not for long. There's work to be done and a life to be lived.

Deadtime

The water was as black as the sky that night they slipped me into the river. Concrete choked my ankles. I felt like a Subbuteo player, my feet fixed, unmoveable. The water was cold, thick. I hit a shelf of mud and silt. Only by pushing back my head could my face break the surface. Occasionally.

I breathed each time a boat went by, but it wasn't frequent enough. The ripples gained me air just as they threatened to dislodge me. My perch was precarious and the river didn't taste too good. My lungs were bursting.

I was in dead time. It was the week that hangs between Christmas and New Year. The one that feels like limbo because everything—every*one*—is on hold. I don't even shave in that week. Just wait for something to happen. Well, now something was happening but I couldn't say I was keen on it.

The cliché is that life flashes before your eyes, but I didn't have that much time, so I made do with a few choice features. I remembered being a kid, setting traps for birds. I clearly saw my red shorts, striped polo shirt, sandals. Stuff I wouldn't be seen dead in nowadays. The traps were woven, slatted with reeds. A little door fell down when a bird entered.

I'd take one out, its tiny beating heart emulating the quiet frenzy of its wings, fluttering against the palms of my hands.

I used to shoot at old glass bottles with an air gun. Once I picked up those reflective shards and pushed them into the bird's body. Thick droplets of pure red blood bubbled on my fingers.

Then I released the bird, watched it try and fly.

It was a blue bird.

The blue bird of happiness.

*

A week earlier I'd frequented Morgan's bar. It was quiet, the wrong time of day for drinking, but a few bums were there for whom it was always the right time of day. I was one of them. I downed a beer with a whiskey chaser. Asked for another. On the bar stool my gun dug at an angle into my thigh. I kept it there. It reminded me that I carried one. Only just. They had threatened to throw me off the force and at that moment my future was in jeopardy. Two days before Christmas, but it wasn't like I had anyone to feed or any presents to buy. The only person I had in the world to care about was me. And I wasn't the caring kind.

Morgan knew when his customers wanted to talk and when they didn't, so he left me alone for a while. But boredom drills a hole into everyone, and when there was no one left to serve he came over and asked me a question.

"So, Mordant. What's what?"

"You've heard the word on the street. You probably know more than I do."

He looked from side to side. As if there was someone in the bar who would care.

"I've heard you've taken a bribe or two and been found out."

"You heard right, but the information is wrong. It was a loan. Just a measly loan."

"All the same to the men up above."

I nodded and ordered another drink. I guess it was. They'd been trying to pin something on me for a while. Once a malcontent, always a malcontent. Of course, it had gotten worse since Rebecca Carlson showed up. If I knew who her connection was on the force then I'd be closer to sorting myself out. But life ain't always easy, and it would take another couple of shots to see things skewed, the way they needed to be.

*

A pile of dirt in my parents' back yard. Some ants. A stick.

Jiggle the stick in the hole and the ants come up. *Help us, the sky is falling.* Those red shorts again. Worn this time with a red string vest. Only in the yard. I imagined them climbing out of an hourglass, the descending dirt losing them time.

Sticking out of my back pocket, my slingshot. Pebbles nearby.

Ant apocalypse.

Once, when I was looking out of the window, no doubt

contemplating the ants, I saw a blue bird pecking at the ground. That's when I got my idea for the traps.

Rebecca Carlson was my blue bird. She flew in from Missouri and made a nest with Piccoli. He was a small-time gangster that I'd been trying to trap for some time. I saw my way in with Rebecca. She was his weak spot. No. They say love is blind. She was his blind spot. And if I stood right behind her, he wouldn't be able to see me.

His front was a milkshake bar just outside Little Italy. The building was old but the canopy was new. The stools were bright shiny plastic in primary colours. The white bar pristine. Piccoli employed a guy who could slide those shakes down to the end of the bar so they frothed up when they reached their destination. That guy was the main man, but the money went to the two waitresses who took more than tips out the back. He had other rackets on the side: extortion, drugs, the usual. You pull him up and he'd swear he was clean, but the only clean operation he ran was money laundering.

I turned up there one day. Solo. Rebecca had been there a week and already she was off limits to everyone else. Long red hair, blue eyes, hips that shook more than the shakes. I watched her setting up tables, rearranging the inside of the milk bar to suit *her* needs, not his. She continued. Giving orders, turning to Mr Milk Shake Man and winking, keeping everyone sweet. But she was an iron fist in a silk glove.

I sucked on my banana shake through a straw. I imagined my arteries clogging with no one to suck it out of me. The phone rang out back and she stopped to answer it.

Snatches of conversation. How much did I need to hear?

"No really, give it up."

And.

"Well, till we meet again."

She was flustered. I could tell. I followed her out of the bar and two blocks away grabbed her arm and held it. She wore a light blue blouse over a stiff white skirt. Tan tights. I didn't wonder then, but I do now, how glass would look like pushed under her skin.

*

The ants weren't the start of it. I had been drawn to the ants because I had been drawn to the yard by the smell. We'd not long moved to the area. No one knew me at school. No one wanted to know me. Maybe it was the red shorts. The back yard was a mess. Most of the stuff was from the previous owner. I found out later that he'd left in a hurry. Car tyres were hidden in thick grass. I fell over one once and cut my knee. The graze stayed for days. The red-speckled skin reminded me of the canal marks on the surface of Mars. In those days, Mars seemed just as far as New York.

There was a rusted swing out back I'd been warned not to play on. A slide at a tilt, similarly so. The ground was uneven, desperate. Later my father would lay fresh turf, surround the house with a picket fence. But he didn't need to do any work clearing the yard. That was done for him.

When I grabbed Rebecca's arm I caught a whiff of perfume. I didn't know the name but I recognised the smell. Immediately, I needed her.

That hadn't been my intention. But then I never have the best intentions.

I steered her into an alleyway. Flashed my ID. Threw the cigar I'd had clamped in the corner of my mouth into a trashcan. Then kissed her hard, once, on the lips.

"Now we gotta deal before we have to say a word. Get it?"

She nodded.

I released her arm and she smoothed down her clothes. Not that I'd rumpled them. She did it to accentuate her body. She didn't need to do that either. My eyes roved her curves. She had me just as deeply as I had her. The die had already been cast.

"Here's what we're gonna do," I said, as though we'd known each other for months. "You're gonna keep an eye on Piccoli for me, and I'm gonna keep quiet about that kiss. Don't keep a diary, keep it all up here." I tapped her forehead, leaving my fingerprint in the residue of her foundation. "When you have enough, you come to me."

Her voice was cold, clear. "What information do you want?"

"Drugs. Everything else I'll turn a blind eye to."

"And how do you know I'll cooperate?"

I kissed her again. My teeth bit her lips. She tried to pull away, laid little punches against my chest. After a while I blew air in her lungs til she couldn't breathe back.

Then I released her.

"Because I know what you're like," I said. Then left her, there in the alleyway.

*

Sometimes I gambled. Sometimes it paid off.

Sometimes you got a smell of something and you knew the taste of it and what it looked like. You knew how it would feel in your hand, how it would sound. Sometimes one of the senses is enough to inform on all five.

Male blue birds are darker than females. Camouflage. Seen from any direction they blend into the sky. I thought that was me, but it must have been a grey day. The male's call includes soft warbles of *jeew* or *chir-wi* or the melodious song *chiti WEEW wewidoo*. That wasn't me. My call was loud and long and meant to make an impact. Only it made too much of an impact. Truth was, even before I kissed her I was lost.

It had been two months before Christmas.

Water filled my lungs.

Five months before another Christmas I found the body in the back yard. One of the neighbours' dogs had been digging, scrabbling away at the earth which was barer than the rest. I threw stones at it til one hit and it yelped and went back over the fence. I later learned never to throw a stone at a dog. I dug with my own hands, finding the loose earth a comfort, like helping my mother make dough. Until my fingers sank into decomposed flesh and the smell really hit me. That night I scrubbed my hands raw and never bit my fingernails again.

When I kissed Carlson, it was like kissing a corpse.

When Mariner 4 flew past Mars on July 14, 1965, providing the first close-up photographs of another planet, it showed a planet that was already dead.

When Rebecca took that phone call I knew she was duping Piccoli. If she took him out and handed him to me then she wouldn't be snitching her true benefactor. She thought she was

97

killing two birds with one stone. But I knew that if she were that way inclined she wouldn't last long in her little trip from Missouri. Double crossers have a habit of being double crossed. Yet she was pretty, she might survive. In another age she'd be called one word. A dame.

Some people thought dames were worth dying for.

When my father got old he lost the use of his legs. Stairs were impossible. One time I phoned my mother and she said she'd bought him an electric chair. To get him from the downstairs to the upstairs. I didn't have the heart to contradict her because truth was he wasn't long off dead.

An electric chair also took our former neighbour. Although my guess is that it took him downwards rather than upwards. The girl hadn't turned twenty-one. She'd been raped and stabbed. I'd had my hands in her rotten breasts before I'd ever touched a live girl's. I soiled myself as I ran back to the house.

Dirt, ants, blue birds. Anything that was coming out of the ground or that fed off the ground.

Who knows what makes a cop a cop. But I was cleaning the streets, getting the crap out of the ground. Sometimes all I did was throw it up in the air and wait for it to come back down. Sometimes I tinkered with it. I should have tasted earth on Rebecca's lips, but they were red and instead I tasted Mars.

*

Someone in the force was paying Rebecca to spy on Piccoli. I should have known it. And that someone had connections—had *made* connections. Connections that I neither had nor made. I'd been too clever, muddied my own waters. I hadn't been clever enough.

Sometimes it just takes a dame with a figure. You take that figure and you double it, add it, subtract it, multiply it by how many times it means something to you and divide it by the difference in your age. Then you're back to the figure you first thought of. You're always back to that figure.

Rebecca would call me, give me information. I lapped it up as she hit me with stones. I could smell her perfume on my pillow at night, I spread her legs wide in my dreams. Her name played games in my mouth. *Rebecca. Becca. Becky.* A dead bluebird is a symbol of disillusionment, of the loss of innocence. Of transformation from the younger and naive to the older and wiser. I was blinded by the glass that she was made of.

My mother died and it turned out that the house was a dud. Remortaged to the hilt from her retirement home costs. What kind of guy doesn't pay for his mother's funeral. By now I was only gunning for Piccoli so I could keep appointments with Rebecca, which never held the intensity of that kiss. Somehow she found out about it, dropped me a few bundles. Next thing you know my mother is buried and her headstone's all shiny. Next thing you know and the cash is traced back to Piccoli.

And the next thing you know is that the slingshot is pointed at me.

They caught up with me after Christmas. In that dead time between then and New Year. It was never going to be a New Year for me. The previous ten years were just old years recycled. I had a date with Rebecca for one of those nights, but unsurprisingly she never showed. Instead four goons bundled me into the back of the car and I was beaten up cinematically at the wharf. All angles and black and white stills. My lips swollen as though injected with collagen. Some dames out in Hollywood paid top dollar for what I got for nothing. Even though I was expected to pay for it.

Lights in my eyes, maybe masks on their faces. I shot off a few wisecracks that only saw life as mumbles. I tried to remember details. The metal sliding doors, the rows of fish hooks, the cracked hull of a boat, the sloshing of the cement mixer. The plastic bucket they put my feet in was red.

I was wheeled out of the yard. Something blue in the corner of my vision, which—three hundred and sixty degrees later —was no longer there. Then the cold of the water, the stink of the river. Something was dead in there and it wasn't yet me.

I gulped another breath. Loosened one foot. These guys were amateurs who'd left my shoes on.

Another splash. Rebecca whipped passed me. Downwards. A scream caught in her throat released as a bubble. The water too murky to imagine the rest but I did. Stilettos can't slip off the same way as brogues.

I worked out my other foot, caught a breath on a wave, ducked my head and swam underwater.

*

Kovacs told me later that it was swimming that had almost killed me. They were onto the goons less than a minute after Rebecca hit the water. I told him that was several minutes too late. When they found me I was sluggish, coughing up pink frothy sputum that could have graced any strawberry shake. In my confused state I

100

tried to swing a few punches. In my conscious state I wished some had hit.

I spent New Year in hospital, paid for by the force. I wish I could say pretty nurses surrounded me but their budget didn't stretch that far. I fobbed off the loan as part of the case, and was sailing so close to the wind that my cigar blew out.

When I was able to swallow another shot down at Morgan's I was wise enough to know I hadn't been expected to escape. Letting Rebecca and myself sink wouldn't have only sealed the case, but also the link back to the force. Someone above me was still on my back. Someone who couldn't yet risk a second strike. If I knew who that someone was I would have told them not to bother. I'd had all my strikes and already wanted out. Sometimes happiness can be found in the simplest of things. Like a blue bird's song, a clean kiss, being tucked up in bed. Just living a simple life.

So this is where I got out. I'd had enough of being submerged in the underworld. I didn't want to remain in limbo. In that dead time between nothing happening and waiting for something to happen. And I'd certainly had enough of the river. I didn't even want water in my scotch.

Not that I ever did. Although they say there were once rivers on Mars.

Ennui

Solange leaves her apartment dressed in a black leather skirt that stops at her thighs. She steadies herself on the side of the doorway as she steps to the pavement. Her hand traces the edges of tiny tiles: pale browns and blues, nondescript. Over her shoulder a green clutch bag is made of feathers and fur. Her blonde hair curves on her neck, drapes over her black cardigan which is patterned at the breast and sleeves with silver swirls.

She nods to the man on the corner, who follows her with his gaze as she walks. Her heels teetering on the pavement. Tiny balances.

From the pavement oak trees break through the concrete and urge skywards. Their roots buckle her way.

In 1878, the photographer Eadweard Muybridge used fifty cameras to prove all four hooves of a horse are off the ground at one point during a gallop.

Solange turns onto the Rue des Archives.

She reaches into her bag and pulls out a single cigarette. Leaning towards a young man she genuflects and he lights her smoke. She nods her head, and he watches her as she continues to walk.

Overnight, when the UFO approached Paris, the city became tinged in milky blue and orange light as though it were twilight. Solange looked out of her apartment window and viewed a hazy opaqueness that seemed impenetrable.

Now, as she regards those who pass her on the street, it is as though the UFO has shrouded Paris in a fog of ennui and numbing complacency, rendering the inhabitants blank and even a little alien-looking themselves.

"Salut!"

The bottom of her skirt rubs against the tops of her stockings.

An arm waves back at her, disappears within traffic. Solange shrugs, turns left onto the Rue de la Verrerie, pulls smoke from the cigarette in her mouth, blows it away so it heads up.

It dissipates, merging with the air around her face, absorbs.

Her heels click on the pavement like the sound of a determined child using an old-fashioned typewriter. In the sky above her the UFO dominates the city, but whilst a pancake-shaped shadow should cloud Paris the sun illuminates the scene. Light will always find a way.

Solange shakes her head to one side so her hair reveals her neck in profile. She runs a hand through it, accentuates the skin. Tiny beads of sweat punctuate her. She watches pedestrians pass by, most with their heads to the ground. Those looking upwards wear dark glasses so she cannot see if their eyes are open or closed. She is aware it is all about perception.

Again she turns left, along the Rue des Moussy. Buildings

pass by her as though it is they who are moving and not she. Cars crawl. Whereas sometimes the sun makes everything slow liquid today it is different. She rolls up her left sleeve to regard her watch but is confronted with a thin strip of lighter skin.

Briefly, a flicker of a frown creases her forehead. Her lips are lightly-paled, her eyebrows etched cleanly. Her blue eyes can't hold a gaze. The muscles in her neck define the sides of her throat. She decides to look up. Can't.

Shortly she turns left onto the Rue Sainte-Croix de la Bretonnerie. She has made a full circle, or rather a shaky rectangle, closer to a rhombus. She approaches her apartment. Leans a hand on the pale tiles again. Pushes the tip of her cigarette into the cracks. Obliterates some grout with ash. Black on white. Entering her apartment she walks through into the living area and stands before the window before the sky before the UFO.

Slowly, she draws the curtains closed.

*

Francine stands beside a tree in the Jardin du Luxembourg. She sighs and a breeze which until then was inconsequential emulates her. She shudders. She moves away from the tree and stands by a metal lamppost moulded with a coat of arms and set into the ground within a circle of cement. She rests against it, then holds it. Her red-painted fingernails follow the curves of the mould, traces patterns which she doesn't think to recognise.

She is dressed for warm autumn weather. A long-sleeved brown woollen dress stops at her thighs. The belt is purely decorative. Boots the same colour as the dress rise to a couple of centimetres beneath her knees. A thick pair of lighter-brown tights completes her ensemble.

The previous evening, when the UFO ascended over the city, she was turning tricks in the park. On her knees, her mouth full, her eyes looking upwards, she saw the shape punctuate the darkness with more darkness. She kept looking, kept the rhythm going. Grass blades patterned her tights when she stood, spitting into a tissue. She stayed there until the next client edged his way through the night's shadow, reaching out for trees to mark his way, to steady him.

Now she leaves the park and finds herself on the Rue de Vaugirard. She turns left, follows the road around the edge of the park. Her long brunette hair flows out behind her as though caught in an updraft.

Unlike Solange, she is not afraid to look overhead. She tries to reconcile her abstract, intellectual knowledge with real, tangible, human understanding.

The UFO is silent.

She passes a couple arguing softly on the corner of the Rue Guynemer. She finds herself wondering what they are saying, walks slower to catch a sentence.

All dialogue is imperfect.

What was it you were trying to tell me?

Why do you love Paul and not me?

I don't love Paul; Madeleine does.

Oh, sure. Why?

I don't want to talk about it. Besides, it's none of your business.

Don't you like going out with boys?

Francine walks beyond earshot. She keeps walking, turns

105

left onto the Rue Auguste Comte. Her arms hang bleakly by her sides. Her dress has no pockets and she has forgotten to carry her bag. The bag contains her credit cards, everything. She is without identity, free. She takes another left, then another, and before she knows it she is back in the park.

She finds a place on the grass that has lost its morning dew. Sits with her legs underneath her, her knees pointing west. Does nothing more. Sits. Stares. Listens.

*

Solange is lying on the couch in her apartment. Outside the traffic has increased. She hears it yet cannot differentiate the noises. Like conversation in a crowded room they become more than individual sounds. The dichotomy between words and sounds blurs. Under her closed eyes everything becomes one. A mass of existence. She lies there and tries to just *be*.

Something comes to her. She was supposed to be somewhere else.

The presence of life is too heavy for her. She can feel it pushing her into the couch, the fabric leaving indentations on her skin, temporary tattoos, pictures in Braille for the blind.

She thinks of fingers on her body, reading her curves. The curtains over the window fluctuate. A breeze cools her skin. She opens her eyes. Sees nothing. Wants to see nothing.

After a while, she opens her legs.

The telephone rings. Solange listens to its plea.

After a short while the tone, whilst exactly the same, takes on an urgency it doesn't really have. She knows she is personalising the object. It isn't really shouting at her, insisting she leave the sofa, getting wilder and madder with each ring. As she acknowledges this the sound becomes uniform, until eventually it stops altogether.

She sits up. Can't help but feel a part of her has been taken.

When she walks to the window, a few moments later, the curtains are still. She draws them open. Unlatches the window. Opens the glass outwards and into the day. The vacuum inside her becomes filled, and in an involuntary motion her left hand touches her stomach.

The UFO has become another building in the sky. She steps onto her balcony, suspended over the street below. To her left she sees her neighbour, also standing on his balcony, and beyond him, also to her left, is his neighbour. She notes that both of their faces show the same dazed expression tinged with a hint of finality, as if they are floating in a sterile world of hastily-built concrete box buildings and artificiality, waiting for it all to crumble at any moment.

*

Francine slides her legs straight, shifts onto her back, lies prone in the park with her gaze only skywards, looking into the belly of the UFO.

Just as sunlight finds its way through the structure, so can she perceive the sky beyond. Simultaneously she sees the UFO and sees the sky. She shields her eyes, puzzles the puzzle. Realises she isn't seeing through it, just that both views exist at the same time.

When she tries to focus, tries to determine what substance the UFO is made of, tries to distinguish patterns and possible doors, she finds herself looking at trees, her head to one side without any discernible trace of movement.

Her eyelids are shadowed in light brown. Her lips are full, slightly parted. She turns again to look at the UFO, but try as she might she can't really see it. Unlike objects which we only notice exist when we turn our attention to them, the UFO becomes less real when it is seen.

Her left hand reaches over her head. She folds a blade of grass between her fingers as she slowly opens her legs. Francine creates a star-shape with her body. A grass angel.

When she closes her eyes the noise of the traffic increases in proportion with the loss of one sense and the heightening of another. The warmth of the sun creates miniscule cracks amongst the foundation on her cheeks. To follow them would be to route an unknown planet. Tracery paths and canals on Mars.

Above the UFO a cloud passes across the sun. Francine shivers, sits up, cross-legged. She places her left hand on her stomach. When she looks around she sees the park is populated. Both men and women are standing or sitting, some leaning against trees. Francine reaches down and unzips her boots, slides her legs out and kicks them off. One boot rests horizontal, the other falls vertical. The cloud passes away from the sun and her toes begin to glow.

She doesn't see any of this.

When she sees this, she doesn't impart meaning to any of it.

*

When Solange leaves her apartment for the second time her feet aren't touching the floor. Like a horse in motion she is captured in an instant in flight. She remains there.

She can't quite remember why she is outside.

On the corner, the man who lit her cigarette is selling newspapers.

She finds she can't read the headline. Or rather, the words won't allow themselves to be read by her.

It is though the newspaper and the words upon it exist in different planes. Solange ponders the syntactical difference between an object's meaning and its significance. There is an implicit duality between the two states which lend her the desire to return to the origin of the fracture. A chill suddenly runs through her and she looks up.

The UFO is exactly the same yet totally different.

She turns left at the next junction.

She is unsure whether people are avoiding her gaze or whether she is avoiding theirs.

She can no longer hear her heels clicking along the pavement. On the Rue de la Verrerie she stops for a coffee.

When she sits, the coffee is already there.

She takes a spoon and stirs. Watches the recurring image of an attenuating vortex swirling within the cup of black coffee, sees the alusion to organic genesis in the pattern's coincidental resemblance to spiral galactical formation and nuclear mitosis.

She shakes her head.

What is all this?

*

Francine stares at the underbelly of the UFO. She makes a decision to no longer prostitute herself. She makes a decision to always be a prostitute. Somewhere in her periphery she understands she will always be prostituted whether she makes a decision or not.

The closer she looks, the clearer she believes she can see a curved *M* on the surface of the UFO.

"Salut!"

She turns her head to one side.

The greeting wasn't aimed at her but she feels part of it. She realises she has been lying on her back, and rises for a second time whilst understanding it could be the first. In the park she has been searching for something, she has always been searching for something.

She recognises one of her clients. He looks different in the daytime with a girl on his arm. Their faces seem pinced, drawn, not haggard but tired. *No longer human*, she thinks; then realises she doesn't know what that means.

She stands. Her head feels sore. She must have been sleeping. When she touches her hair a mild electric shock tingles her fingertips.

There is just enough here, she realises, for humankind to carry itself as normal. Until the time comes that it doesn't need to carry itself at all. Until there is just a state of being, rather than passing moods.

*

That evening, both Francine and Solange look into the sky as the

UFO rises vertically, almost imperceptibly, until they can only determine where it was by looking into the place where it no longer is.

Then, a little later, Solange and Francine realise they are only looking at stars.

Under their breath, they make a wish.

Within days, their stomachs are distended.

Lauren is Unreal

I boarded the train at Nottingham to find it full of football fans. I didn't recognise their tribal colours belonging to any team I knew, but from their cheers and chants it seemed I was with the winning side. Moving quickly through the carriage, my lack of colour causing confusion on some faces, I passed into the next.

There it was just as crowded. Standing room only. But birds of a feather flock together, and again I jostled my way through the hordes, my back pack hitting the shoulder of someone too drunk and elated to care, until finally—several carriages later—I came across one which was more to my liking.

Here they might have been refugees. It felt as though I'd emerged from a battle. Compared to the fans, their expressions were glazed and held little emotion. Woody Allen's *Stardust Memories* came to mind, but then it would, given my background.

I looked ahead and saw a seat was available with a table. I had some work to do. My laptop was in my backpack and I needed to write the lecture for my next class. Cross-dressing in the movies. *Laurel and Hardy. Silence of the Lambs. Priscilla, Queen of the Desert*. It was like shooting fish in a barrel. I could write it in my sleep—if only that was literally rather than figuratively. There was a family at the table, two adults and a girl. Smiling apologetically, as if I had something to apologise for, I slid along the seat opposite them and put my backpack down beside me.

I looked out of the window and saw it was already dark. The clocks had changed the previous weekend, England disjointed temporarily until routine kicked in and it all became familiar again. As a child I'd considered those changes as pivotal, as though life could split in two directions, one containing the extra hour and the other not. But now I just complained about the darkness signalling the onset of winter. Just thirty-one, but already part of an older generation.

I opened my laptop, and as I waited for everything to load I glanced up at the family. It suddenly struck me as odd that they were three abreast. In these cramped seats that was something of an achievement. The father sat closest to the aisle, indifferent, looking down the centre of the train as though he were expecting someone. Mother sat in the middle of the group, her daughter's head rested on her shoulder. Her expression seemed faraway, perhaps dreaming of better times. She stroked her child's fair hair with long fingers.

Both parents paid no attention to me, but I couldn't look directly at the girl because she was staring. She wasn't as young as I'd first thought, probably late teens, but she didn't appear a typical teenager. Her mother's attention would be anathema to most of that generation. Even so, like most teenagers, her ears were plugged with music I could only hear as a continuous buzz.

I tried to work, but like a moth to a flame I couldn't stop

113

glancing at her. I found myself typing random words to make it look like I was working, but each time I looked up she was still watching me, as though she were waiting for it. For a moment I felt as though something were passing between us, a secret. And whilst I knew I was reading too much into it, part of me wanted to prolong it.

Her skin was pale, almost translucent. It struck me that she might be ill, which could explain the attention of her mother and the non-attention of her father. Comfort and distance. Her face was oval, eyes blue, the barest of eyebrows. She wore no make-up, her naturally pink lips were thin. Freckles spotted her cheeks as though she had been painting with a stiff brush. She wasn't attractive, yet she wasn't unattractive. She was compulsive.

I speculated. I imagined they were taking her home; considered an illness, suicide attempt, lost love. I wondered whether she would smile back if I were to smile at her. I wondered whether I *should* smile at her. I wondered *why* I wanted to smile at her.

Was there some kind of kinship, or was it fabricated because we were bubbled together on the same train for a couple of hours in a fantasy world of my own making. Surely once we arrived then reality would reassert itself, like the clocks going forward in summer time, and any interest we had in each other would dissipate?

These were questions that populated, crowded, my mind during the first hour of the journey.

I tried again with my work, but the title alone gazed back at me from the screen. I had to deliver by ten the following morning. Yes, I could busk it, but I wanted something structured.

Mimetic nods, if nothing else.

I watched her hands. The skin was delicate, her movements slow. They lifted, made movements in the air, touched each other, fingertip to fingertip. It was then I realised she was signing.

I glanced across to her mother, who reached into a bag and pulled out a packet of crisps. She opened them and placed them on the table. The girl reached in, took one, and popped it into her mouth.

I looked away, ashamed now. She obviously had at least one disability and I shouldn't have been staring. Maybe she also had learning difficulties, which might explain her apparent interest in me. Then I reminded myself the interest was in my head.

I worked again, made a list of bullet points for the lecture. Now they ran through me like a dose of salts, as though the dam to my imagination had been lifted. When I dared to look at the girl again, her parents were asleep.

At first, I thought she was also sleeping. I could still hear the music humming in her head, too indistinct to determine whether it was dance or indie, hip-hop or R'n'B. Her eyes were closed, the lids so thin that I could almost see the blueness beyond. She wore a thin, white top, and her chest was rising and falling beneath it. Without the need to look away, I watched her for some time. And, as I did, a smile shaped her lips. Faint at first, then broad, revealing clean white teeth.

I glanced down as she opened her eyes. Then her leg nudged mine and I looked back up. She was rooting around in a drawstring bag—it looked handmade, crocheted and patterned with daisies. She pulled out a notepad and pen, scribbled something fast, then tore out the page cleanly, slipping it across the table to me. Face down.

I reached over and took it. How couldn't I have done? Then flipped it over.

I'm not deaf—Lauren

A mobile phone number underlined her name. The letters were cutely curved, typical female. I realised my heart was pounding. She smiled again, then raised a finger to her lips. Again, her leg touched mine under the table. It was a light pressure, which remained there for the remainder of the journey, and indeed, for some time afterwards.

At Norwich, the final destination, I watched them leave. It was a while before I could move. Finally, I closed my laptop and then realised I hadn't saved my notes. Lauren's piece of paper burnt a hole in my pocket as I left the station.

*

It was a week before I phoned her. There was so much to consider. The age difference played on my mind, viewing it from both angles. But also the intention, the reason behind what she had done. I didn't want a relationship, any kind of relationship. I didn't do those. Surely it was the ephemeral nature of our meeting which was the only appeal—reality would taint it, lose it. I got bored in relationships, and I didn't think it would be fair to get bored of Lauren.

The signing bothered me. She wasn't mute, she could hear the music. I considered sign language as an evolutionary

116

step, one so that teenagers could always hear their music. Ridiculous, but a possible explanation?

I coasted through the week's lectures, although whether my disinterest showed itself to the bored students that took my lessons it was hard to tell. I used to pride myself on my enthusiasm, my *Dead Poet's Society* method of teaching, my willingness to transform young minds. But after a while I realised I was only trying to recapture my youth, to become accepted amongst a group of people who didn't feel that connection. And once I saw how sad that was, all the energy, *all* the positive direction, bled out of me. I knew my stuff—that hadn't changed —but how it was received became immaterial.

I called her Monday lunchtime.

Her voice, new to my ears, was light, girly. I couldn't quite connect it to the girl on the train.

"Hello?"

"Hi? Is that Lauren? I'm Richard. I was sitting opposite you on the train last Sunday." I faltered. The line was quiet. "You gave me your number."

"*Richard.*" I could almost feel my name rolling around her mouth, her mind, as she considered it. "Of course. Richard. Would you like to meet?"

I paused. What *was* it that I was after? A connection? But what was it that *she* was after?

"Yes. Yes, I would like to meet."

Was she smiling at me down the phone? "You sound unsure."

"No, I am sure. Truly."

Truly. What kind of word was that?

"Okay, how about this evening? I finish college at five. Pick me up from there?"

"City College? For coffee?"

"Sure."

"Okay."

"Okay, Richard. See you then."

She hung up.

When I replaced the receiver I saw it was wet. So was my forehead. I wasn't sure if the unknown terrified or excited me. In my mind she was a blank canvas, but in hers she was a fully formed person. For Lauren, *I* was the blank canvas.

Then an absurd thought crossed my mind. What if she were paying her way through college through sexual favours? *Would you like to meet?* It had sounded perfunctory, almost businesslike. I pushed the thought out of my mind. Lauren wasn't like that. *Lauren wasn't like that?* But I didn't know anything about her at all.

The remainder of the afternoon passed in a daze.

*

Driving from the university I took the inner ring road. The traffic was light, my senses heightened through anticipation. As I turned onto Ipswich Road I realised I would be approaching City College from the wrong direction. I'd have to drive past, then take the roundabout, and come back the other side. I wondered if I'd glimpse Lauren as I did so.

A sense of life in reverse permeated me. Always on the wrong side of the road, the wrong age, the wrong choices. It started raining and I wondered if she'd wait.

I drove past the College but couldn't see her, then drummed my fingers along the steering wheel as I got caught up in traffic. By the time I was heading in the right direction I was already ten minutes late.

I saw her immediately. She was standing with a group of girls, the back of her jacket pulled up in an attempt to cover her hair from the rain. I pulled up beside her, waited for the laughter directed at the saddo who'd been taken in by her apparent innocence. But Lauren just nodded at her friends, then was suddenly beside me in the car, dripping wet, looking over as though everything were natural, and with a smile on her face that was both expectant and hesitant.

"Hi." The voice now married to the face still didn't fit. "Where are we going?"

"I'm not sure. The weather's not great."

"Nearest place for coffee is Notcutts."

"The garden centre?"

"Sure, why not?"

I shrugged and drove. Silence permeated us. Lauren seemed tiny within my car, huddled into herself for warmth, for dryness. Her jacket was too short and thin for the weather. She wore a skirt and patterned tights; semi-circles ran a path on her knees.

"Cold?"

She nodded. "A bit."

"We'll soon be there."

"I know."

I wanted to ask why she wanted to meet, but I couldn't.

The garden centre was almost deserted. It was nearly closing time. The dining area was huge, as big as an aircraft hangar with high ceilings and white walls. Totally antiseptic and uninviting. I ordered an espresso and a hot chocolate for Lauren, and when I took them over to where she was sitting I saw her headphones were plugging her ears.

She smiled disconcertingly, kept the music on. What would we do now? My espresso was too hot to drink. I was tense. What was I doing here anyway? I had my thesis to write on contemporary Australian film. The idea was to work up from *Picnic at Hanging Rock* and then check IMDb to get a feel for stuff that was upcoming. Again, this work was easy for me—too easy —but it needed to be done. I still wasn't sure if I found her attractive.

Finally she pulled the earphones from her head. The music stopped automatically. She smiled again and reached for her hot chocolate with delicate fingers.

"So," she said, "What are we doing here?"

I shook my head. "I don't know, really. Do you?"

She shrugged. "I like being impulsive." She sipped her drink. "What do you listen to?"

"Listen to?"

"In your earphones. Voices in your head. I'm sure you have some. Everyone does. Although there wasn't anything playing in your car."

"I'd turned the radio off so I could think."

"Okay."

She took another sip of her drink, then fell silent. Waiting.

"I listen mostly to 80s music," I said. "That's where my teenage years were forged. The Smiths, The Three Johns, Pop Will Eat Itself. Lately, The Beautiful South."

She nodded. I couldn't tell if she approved or was amused or what.

"I don't listen to much that is recent," I added. "What do you listen to?"

"I listen to you," she said, and smiled.

I laughed. "I know you're listening to me now," I said. "What else do you listen to?"

"Oh, a lot of different things. You wouldn't know them."

Another silence descended, uncomfortable this time. Was this a game? I still felt that pressing connection to her I wasn't sure how to handle.

"Do you want to sleep with me?"

She caught me off guard. But I bit back a knee-jerk answer, then found to my surprise there wasn't one. I considered it for a few moments, and when I answered I felt a surge of relief in release.

"No."

She smiled. "Good answer. That's just what I wanted to hear."

*

Lauren moved in with me one week later. It was all very chaste. She had her room and I had mine. We had an odd relationship. I wasn't even sure if I could describe it as such. Most evenings we chatted, often over a glass of wine. The conversation always

121

steering my way, even when I tried to turn it the other. Not that I didn't enjoy talking about my life. I embellished here and there, but gradually felt I had more worth than I had done in ages.

When we did talk about her it was never specific. She never said what she was studying, although I gleaned it was media-based. She'd taken an interest in my film theory work, seemingly absorbing my views on Godard and Besson and Jeunet. But she wasn't studying film *per se*. I had a feeling it was more social than that.

One evening she was sitting on the opposite sofa, her legs tucked underneath her and her earphones on. I'd arrived late from university with a kebab, which she declined. She usually ate alone in her room. There was almost no meat on her, but she seemed healthy enough. I'd had a rough day, some vigorous questioning on what I really felt about *Delicatessen* had left me drained. Whilst I knew the film inside out, I couldn't focus. I'd only discussed it the previous evening with Lauren, but my opinion had somehow slipped away.

On the drive home I thought about this in detail. Empty spaces were opening up in my mind. I realised everything we know can always be forgotten. And subjects I'd picked over with her now seemed indistinct.

So when I saw her on the sofa, my kebab trailing from my mouth, tiredness kicked in and I didn't want to talk about myself anymore. I had a sense that doing so would somehow lose a little bit more of me.

"Lauren?"

She looked up. Her blue eyes open, receiving me.

I wondered what it was she saw.

"Can you hear me?"

She nodded. "It's low. I can hear you perfectly."

I fought my annoyance that I didn't have her undivided attention, but continued anyway.

"What exactly are you studying?"

She sighed. "Anthropology. I told you Richard. I'm studying people and their cultural references."

"Give me an example. Please."

"I created a street survey where I asked people what they were listening to through their headphones. I collected their musical tastes, age groups, gender, and produced a report based on those demographics. It was clear to me that people of different ages listen to different music—of course, that's not unexpected—but also that they defined themselves by that music. Almost a two-way process—mutually symbiotic, if you will—because the music stays alive when someone listens to it. That was the main push behind my thesis."

I wasn't sure it was much of a thesis, but I reminded myself she wasn't doing a degree.

"So," I said, taking another kebab bite, "how would you class yourself? What group do you come into?"

"Me? I don't fall into any of the groups."

I laughed. "You must do. What are you listening to now?"

"You."

I wasn't in the mood for this. I put the remainder of the kebab in the bin, and wondered whether this was going to be our first argument. Then I realised the very thought meant I considered we were in a relationship. I wondered what she really

123

wanted, and why I'd never asked. How easily I'd invited her here; how easily she had come.

I wondered how easily I could make her go.

I couldn't focus, so I went over to the fridge and took out a beer. Closing the door I noticed the coloured magnetic letters that had been a 'free gift' through the mail a few years ago. I'd forgotten what they were advertising because I didn't take up on it, but I'd stuck the letters onto the fridge and occasionally rearranged them. Their use was limited because there were no duplicate letters. So *Se Da* was my shorthand for *See Dad.* Other things, such as *bread*, made more sense.

I hadn't touched them for a while, but now I saw they'd been fiddled with. In the centre of the fridge was the following:

lauren

ich d

I put my hand out, my fingers following the line of the *l*, the cool plastic smooth to my touch. I turned and looked through to the living room. Lauren was stretched out on the sofa, her left leg an l-shape in itself. Suddenly an emotional longing surged through me, something I couldn't place in any sense. Almost a loss, or—more specifically—an impending loss.

I found I wanted to hug her, to tell her everything was okay. But everything *was* okay.

I needed to get some sleep.

I went back into the living room. Lauren's head was turned away from me and I touched her on the shoulder. She jumped and one of the earpieces fell out of her head. I heard a tinny voice without music, but couldn't catch any words. Lauren looked up at me, her eyes glazed, expression displaced. Then the voice stopped and she blinked and everything returned to normal.

"I'm getting an early night."

She smiled. "You don't look well."

"Just tired. See you tomorrow."

"Okay."

She replaced her earpiece and sank back into the sofa.

*

I woke up and wasn't sure if I was dreaming. My head felt tight, as it sometimes does when I keep the central heating on during the winter. My ears were buzzing as though attuned to the dead tone of a telephone. My eyes were sticky, sealed. I rubbed them.

In the darkness of the room I saw a darker shadow. *Lauren?* I blinked and it was gone. I felt pressure then, on both sides of my head. I couldn't move but I couldn't tell if I were trying. When I drifted back to sleep it was with a feeling of utter helplessness.

When I woke in the morning I felt determined she had to go.

I needed my old life back. The one which contained all my memories intact and unrelinquished. We weren't a couple, but she had coupled me, made me feel whole for a while; but really there was no reason for her to be around. She highlighted my deficiencies, gave nothing in return.

Not only that but we met on a whim, an impulse, and

there was no real connection between us other than one imagined. And it certainly wasn't physical. Having her here was a barrier to bringing someone else back home. Plus she wasn't contributing financially. She might be a light eater but it still made a difference to my budget.

All these thought processes went through my mind in the full knowledge I couldn't kick her out.

The house was quiet. I wasn't sure if she were still there or at college. I tried to work on a lecture I had to conduct that afternoon. *Motifs and Metaphors in Cocteau's Orphée*. But the laptop screen stayed blank as I realised I couldn't focus, couldn't remember the movie even though Lauren and I had watched it not less than a few days previously.

I ran a hand through my hair, my scalp felt tender. Maybe I was coming down with something. I decided to make some hot milk, then realised how childish that would be. Nevertheless, I was already at the fridge and stopped only when I saw the letters.

They were still present, in the same sequence, but what struck me today was the absence contained in mine.

Mutually symbiotic.

Yesterday, Lauren's arrangement of the letters had touched me. Today, physically, mentally, I felt I was peeling away. I touched my forehead, wondered if I were ill. Then I remembered I'd thought that earlier, or was it yesterday, or the day before? Why wasn't I doing anything about it?

I touched the *c* in my name with a fingertip. The curvature was indicative of a half-life. The half not lived out of the half of my life I had lived already. I shook my head. My thoughts jumbled like mixed-up letters. Again, I had the feeling I had been trying to justify my existence by the association or approval of others. Wasn't that why I moved Lauren in here, to substantiate me?

The more I looked at the letters, the more I wanted to rearrange them. To readdress the balance. To complete myself. I started to bring the *r* down towards the start of my name, and then gave a jolt as another hand touched mine, moved it back up.

I turned to face Lauren. She didn't look as pale as usual. Her hand was warm to the touch. She was dressed for college, and I noticed her bag on the kitchen table although I hadn't heard her come into the room. She pulled my fingers away from the letters with a firm grip.

"Watch," she said.

She rearranged the letters in her name: *Unreal.*

Then she changed my letters: *Dickhead.*

My legs buckled. "That's not right," I mumbled, as though I were concussed.

Too many letters. There weren't that many letters.

Lauren's hand was in mine. She led me over to the table. Something slipped into my ears and my head fell silent. Lauren sat opposite me and signed. Some part of my brain knew the sign and understood. *Listen to this.*

There was a light buzz, a tingling in my ears. Then:

her skin looks pale translucent i wonder if she's ill
her leg is touching mine
i don't know how i feel about her
stays alive when someone listens
really has to go

I felt the earphones leave my head and Lauren placed

127

them in her ears. She seemed to listen for a long time, far longer than it could have been, but I heard nothing, not even the sound of my own breathing. When she stood up and picked up her bag, I realised it was her suitcase.

She left without a backwards glance and I watched her go.

Although when I say watched, I'm not sure I comprehend the meaning of the word.

I'm not even sure I know the meaning of *word*.

I look at my hands. Make movements with them. Movements I don't fully understand.

PhotoTherapy©

Spencer understood people were easy to fool, but until he met Jamieson he hadn't realised how easy.

"See that guy?" Spencer pointed along the hallway to a secure room at the far end. The interior was black, only two clenched fists around the bars indicating a presence.

"Sure."

"Ripped his mother's head off with those hands."

"Really?"

"Then ate it."

"Huh?"

A new recruit to the Criminal Rehabilitation Bureau, Jamieson came straight out of college with no practical experience. Spencer suspected he was a virgin in other areas too. With those thin-framed, thick-lens glasses and short-cropped hair he looked like an extra from *One Flew Over The Cuckoo's Nest*. Although being typically acerbic at having a new recruit assigned to him, Spencer knew it didn't matter how Jamieson might appear. He'd get the piss ripped out of him anyways.

129

"So, this your first time in a secure unit?"

"Well, I spent a work experience month at Freethorpe . . . "

Spencer laughed. His laugh didn't have much humour in it.

"Freethorpe? That nancy boy prison? Hardly prepares you for here."

Jamieson shrugged. He knew all about Spencer and wasn't going to bite. If he kept quiet, Spencer would talk out of boredom. It was a technique he'd seen demonstrated with prisoners at Freethorpe. Even if they *were* only *nancy boys* there.

Spencer opened a door on the right. The locker room. He handed Jamieson a key.

"This is where you put all your personal belongings. All the stuff you don't want nicked by the pickpockets and mass-murderers we have here. Just keep anything valuable at home. Locked in that locker don't mean that it's safe.

Spencer took something metallic out of his pocket. The lock on the adjacent locker opened with a click. He reached inside and pulled out a girlie magazine. Flicked through it: bums and tits flashing before his eyes.

"This is Cedric's locker. You'll meet him later. Remember this."

Spencer thrust the mag back. Shut the door and locked it.

Jamieson watched. Then opened his own locker without using the key. Placed his rucksack inside. Closed it.

*

Their first job was the rehabilitation of Belmondo.

"I got the photos here," Spencer said.

They were sitting opposite each other at a table in the canteen. Spencer fanned the photos on the sticky surface like a deck of cards.

"Pick one."

Jamieson chose the closest. Turned it over. Three people: no doubt father, mother, and son. The sea as background. The son on the father's back, piggy-style. The mother's hand rested lightly on her son's shoulder. All smiling.

"This is Belmondo, right?"

"Right."

"So, how do they do this?"

"I don't do technology, so it doesn't matter how they do it. What matters is what *we* do *with* it."

Spencer collected the photos, shuffled them, ordered them.

"One at a time. Two weeks and Belmondo will be out. We don't want him re-offending."

"We *can't* have him re-offending," said Jamieson.

"You sound like Cedric."

Cedric wasn't the kind of person you wanted to sound like. But Jamieson knew it wasn't an insult as such, just a knee-jerk reaction to nannying. Anyway, he'd been warned.

Spencer wiped his mouth with a dirty handkerchief that looked like its sole purpose was for mouth-wiping after hamburger meals.

"C'mon. Let's go. And don't say anything."

They walked to the canteen door. Nodded to the guard to let them out. Continued down the corridor. Nodded to the next guard. And so on. Until finally they were outside the interview room.

131

"He'll have been in there thirty minutes already. You can imagine how he'll be feeling. Brace yourself."

Jamieson noticed the grin on Spencer's face as he opened the door.

The room was sparsely furnished. A long table and four chairs stood almost in shadow. Two chairs were vacant, their backs to the door. Two chairs were occupied. A prison warder sat by the door, his hand covering the handle of a revolver. The other chair contained Belmondo. He sat facing them, his hands in his lap, an expression of calm bewilderment on his face.

Jamieson noticed the lines on his skin, wondered how old he was. Late forties, early fifties? Information had been held back as an integral part of his training. In order to understand, he had to come to it clean.

Spencer nodded to Belmondo, pulled up a chair, and sat down. Jamieson did likewise.

"My name's Spencer. This here's Jamieson. He won't say much. He's here to observe. Ignore him if you can."

Belmondo nodded.

He didn't look particularly dangerous.

"You know why you're here?"

Belmondo shook his head.

"For the tape," Spencer said, "that was a negative."

Jamieson looked around for the tape. As far as he could see there wasn't one. Maybe that was the point. He looked back to Belmondo.

"Verbal answers are best," Spencer said. "You know what I'm saying."

Belmondo nodded, checked himself, then said 'yes'. It

132

sounded like the first word he'd spoken in days. Maybe it was.

"We're here to get your memory back."

Spencer felt inside his pocket, pulled out a photo, and placed it on the middle of the table, facing Belmondo. Jamieson looked at it upside-down. It was a similar family scene to the one at the beach. Belmondo was standing, facing the camera, his son in front of him, his hand resting on his son's head. To his right stood his wife. A good foot shorter than Belmondo and a good foot higher than their son. All three were smiling.

"You recognise anyone?"

Belmondo reached out a gnarled tattooed finger and pointed to himself. "This is me, the others I don't know."

Jamieson looked closer, saw that the finger of the Belmondo in the photograph was also tattooed. A snake: its head the fingernail, the body working its way back to the knuckle.

"How would you describe the relationship of the other people in the photo?"

Belmondo shrugged. "They look happy enough."

Spencer pointed to the woman. "This is your wife, Veronica." He pointed to the boy. "This is your son, Aaron."

Belmondo picked up the photo. "I don't see nothing," he said.

*

Another day, another burger. Jamieson watched as Spencer sank his teeth into his food. On his own plate, the flaccid *vegetarian option* looked like it had been pulled from someone's back garden. A few salad leaves, half a carrot sliced sideways, some cucumber. He got the feeling it was designed not to be an option.

Spencer spoke. His mouth full. "You think we're making progress?"

Jamieson thought back to the previous day. This time Belmondo had recognised his family. Although it wasn't surprising. They'd shown him identical photos for the past four days. The drug took everything, but everything could be rebuilt.

"I know what you're thinking," Spencer said. "But it has to be gradual. We have to establish connections in his mind. If it was that easy to remember then there'd be no guilt."

A question rose on Jamieson's lips, then he took it back. Then thought better of it. This was what he was here for.

"I know I'm withheld information so I can see this from Belmondo's perspective, but I just want to know one thing. After these two weeks, will he actually be at the end of his sentence or if he's *rehabilitated* is he going to be set free before his time?"

Spencer sat back. Jamieson thought he was going to reach for his handkerchief, but he used the back of his hand instead.

"There's a lot of prisons nowadays and the country is crowded with them, but there's even more prisoners crowding the prisons. When this works, it works."

"Regardless of his sentence?"

"Regardless." Spencer paused. "Look, for what Belmondo did, he wouldn't ever be going out. *Pathological*, I think that's the word they use. So what do we do? Keep him here, at our expense, for years and years and years? Doped up? Or let him go, safely. You tell me."

Jamieson shrugged. "He seems harmless enough."

Spencer took the photos out of his pocket. Flicked through

them. Seemed to choose one, then thought better of it and put it back. There was a time and a place for everything.

"Let's go."

They went through locked door after locked door after locked door.

Belmondo sat in his chair as though he'd never left it. Jamieson thought he looked a little nervous. He was never self-assured, but under the bewildered expression there seemed to be a thirst for knowledge, coupled with trepidation at what that knowledge might contain.

They sat down opposite. Spencer pulled a photo out of his pocket. Placed it on the table between them.

Belmondo picked it up. Traced his tattooed finger along the face of his wife. Breathed the word *Veronica*.

"How are they?" he asked.

Spencer's face was stoic as usual.

"We were hoping you'd know the answer to that one."

Belmondo shook his head. Clutched his head.

"I don't know anything."

Spencer took another photo out of his pocket. Again, placed it on the table.

"Remember this?"

Belmondo snatched the photo up before Jamieson had the chance to see it.

"Who done this?"

"Why do you think you are here?"

"I don't know. I don't remember anything."

"Look at the photo."

Belmondo threw it on the table. Jamieson snatched a look.

135

Veronica's face had a long blue-black bruise down one side. Her left eye looked like it had been poached.

Spencer picked up the photo and returned it to his pocket. He replaced the space on the table with another.

It seemed to be the same photo, shot at the same angle. Veronica was smiling. There were no bruises on her face.

Belmondo picked it up, looked at it fondly. Mouthed the word *baby*.

The session was over.

*

That night, Jamieson lay in his rented hotel room, staring at the ceiling. If he looked carefully, he could see faces in the nicotine-created whorls. He imagined them looking down at him. Wondering who he was. What new inhabitor he might be out of all the previous inhabitors and the successive inhabitors. At which point had he entered the evolutionary chain and at which point would he leave it.

Just how much did anyone know?

*

"Tell us about your family."

"I met Veronica in High School. She was the sweetest girl there. I couldn't speak to her she was so pretty. One day I took her hand, led her away from her friends. It was like I was sleepwalking, my footsteps leaden, stumbling through syrup. But she walked beside me as light as a ballerina. At the side of the school, leaning against the hot brick, away from prying eyes, I kissed her."

"Tell us about that kiss."

"I remember it as clear as day. It wasn't perfect. My top lip brushed against her teeth, my bottom lip underneath hers. But then we found each other. It was a revelation. My heart didn't beat faster, but ... I can't describe it ... it felt like it was glowing, levitating inside my chest."

"So you dated?"

"Yeh, we dated. You know this right? You know how much in love we were. And when Aaron came along, everything was just perfect."

A series of photos were spread along the table. Telling the story just as Belmondo remembered it.

"I need to know," he said. "I just need to know what happened to them. Where they are."

Jamieson saw heavy pools of water sitting at the edges of Belmondo's eyes, held there only by a skein of tension.

Spencer shook his head. "Can't tell you that. Not today."

Jamieson expected Belmondo to fill with rage, but instead there was only sadness. Where were these psychopathic traits Spencer had told him about? Yet maybe that was the point of all this. To ensure they didn't surface.

In the locker room Spencer opened Cedric's locker, pulled out another girlie magazine, and drew a moustache across a beaming model's face using a thick black marker pen.

"Anyone asks," he said, "and I'll tell them it was you."

*

Jamieson thought about the defaced image on his bus journey home. He thought about the photographs. He thought about Spencer, about the persona he projected. He took off his glasses and popped in his contact lenses. He got off the bus a stop early and entered a strip club.

A girl danced in front of him, wearing only tassles and a thong, but however close she came he knew he still couldn't really see her.

*

The following day when Jamieson entered the canteen Spencer was picking at a salad.

Jamieson nodded at the plate.

"Doctor's orders." Spencer forked greenery into his mouth.

Jamieson wondered when Spencer obeyed doctor's orders.

Belmondo couldn't wait to see the photographs again. He almost pounced on them as if they were the physical embodiments of his family. Tears flowed freely. Whether of joy or of loss Jamieson couldn't tell.

As Belmondo clutched the photos he had already seen, Spencer pulled out five new images. Laid them side by side on the table, as though a photo story told through some girls' magazine.

"Hey, Belmondo. You seen these?"

Jamieson couldn't quite make out the photos from where he was sitting. He rubbed his eyes behind his glasses. Then realised why they were unclear. He'd been expecting more of the same. Happy family photos with whole bodies. But in these photos you really had to look to see that they were people.

138

Had been people.

Belmondo looked. Roared. Swept the photos off the table with one long, powerful movement. Then sank off his chair onto the floor and wept.

Outside, five minutes later, Spencer showed the final photograph to Jamieson.

"We're almost there," he said.

Jamieson knew it was faked. Who could have taken it? Belmondo stood in the middle of the living room, the same living room in which many other happy family photographs had been taken, holding an axe. On the floor in front of him were the dismembered bodies of his wife and child.

"You were expecting this, of course," Spencer grinned.

"It can't be real, can it?"

"Can't it?"

"I mean, who would have taken it?"

"I doesn't matter. Belmondo won't see beyond what he thinks he remembers. From research, we know the final photograph has to be illusory. He has to be *seen* to be there or all the dots won't connect. He has to know it was him."

"But it can't be him, can it?"

"You tell me," Spencer said, "you tell me."

*

Spencer was right. When they showed the final photo to Belmondo he *remembered* everything. The sadness—the guilt—in his eyes was palpable. He bent over double, wracked with sobs, swearing that he would never, ever, do anything so dreadful again.

139

Leaving the interview room, Jamieson knew that he wouldn't. But he remained unconvinced about what he had done in the first place.

He cornered Spencer in the men's room.

"I know my debriefing is tomorrow, but I've got a few questions. You sure you can't tell me now?"

"Well, I'd like to but you know I'm a stickler for the rules."

For Jamieson, that was as good as a confession.

"Why do it this way? Why not work back from the killings and make him see how happy he used to be? Wouldn't that give him hope? That things could be just as good again? Wouldn't that send him out into the world looking for something positive?"

Spencer almost snarled. "It would set him up for a fall. Nothing in life is perfect, you know this. You want him triggered into offending again? Only in absolute despair will his urges be cowed. He's beaten. Defeated. The only way is up. Maybe he'll start putting some value on life, even if it isn't his own."

"Does he get support outside of here?"

"He won't need it."

Jamieson wondered how much support everyone needed.

He grabbed Spencer's arm as he was about to leave.

"So, what was his crime?"

Spencer grinned. "Shoplifting."

Jamieson shook his head, watched Spencer leave and the door close. Then he sat in one of the cubicles and emptied himself.

*

"I remember our first kiss. We sat on the beach. It had rained the previous evening and we hadn't bought a blanket, so whilst the sand was superficially dry damp penetrated our clothing. I was on a promise. The promise was certain. I knew I'd get that first kiss and it was only a matter of when. And in that knowledge I delayed it. Increased the anticipation until such a moment that the kiss itself became inevitable. And when we did kiss, it was perfect, because it couldn't be anything else."

*

Jamieson made his way back to the locker room. Did it matter if Belmondo had committed any crime, or did it only matter if he thought he had? The corridor was dim and deserted. He passed a succession of empty rooms. White flashes illuminated a doorway. As Jamieson reached it a woman and a boy came out. They ignored him, went in the direction he had come.

Jamieson glanced into the room they had left. Saw a sofa, flowered wallpaper, an exercise bike in the corner, a fish tank, a camera.

When Jamieson opened his locker and took out his rucksack, photos fell to the floor. He picked them up, flicked through them. He didn't remember the girl, but he had his arm around her. Funfair lights speckled the background. A candyfloss stall had a crudely-painted, misspelled sign. Giant teddy bears filled row upon row of a rifle-game stall, like spectators watching from a stadium. A skull menaced the frontage of a haunted house ride.

He caught blurred glimpses of himself and Veronica on the walzter.

141

Despite knowing they were false, he still knew they were the best of times.

Red or White

Is she red, is she white?
Is she promised to the night?
—*Trad. circa 1890*

I find myself searching through the dark and daylight hours. Hoping I can find her in both and not only in one. The sun was so good to her, accentuating her looks, her perfect cheekbones, making her raven-dark hair shine with an almost luminescent fluidity. She cannot have lost that, I tell myself, when I am too tired and too scared to remain wandering the dark streets alone. I need her back with me. Back with her old man.

Amanda was the first. I could hardly conceal my disappointment when she was born. I won't deny that I was looking for a son, someone to run the wine shop alongside me, and eventually to take over once I was dead. It took me two years to accept her as my offspring, all the while hoping that my wife, Katherine, would bear another child, one who might be more suited to carrying on the family name. Sometimes I wonder whether it was such a hope that displeased God, or whether my bitter confused rationale leant itself to abuse from another source. Whatever it might have been, it couldn't stifle the anguish I felt when Katherine died in childbirth, and my new son only a few hours after that. The midwife cried openly—she knew us both well —but I kept it tight inside me; fool that I was to think I could hide my grief.

Outside, I can see the red rivers of another sunset streak the horizon. A beautiful sight now that the Machine has cleared our skies, even though this signals the night that I now abhor. A clockwork horse rattles along the cobblestones pulling its black cab, the occupants glimpsed briefly in an embrace as it passes by my window. I open the wooden drawer beside the counter and look at the key to the shop. Dare I close early, start my search for her right now? As if in answer the sun sinks lower over the horizon and casts a shadow inside the shop that temporarily vanishes the key. I sigh, reach into another drawer for a taper, and enter the backroom warmed by the fire. By the time I return with the lantern, the bell over the door has rung, and something is in the shop.

At first I can see nothing, then a shape moves in the shadows, and under the velvet of a black cloak the red silk lining flashes back the light from my lantern, reflecting a gaunt face and thin body. I catch my breath.

"Good evening, sir." My voice is strained, nervy. "May I help you? We're just about to close."

"I'm looking for a red." His voice, contrary to mine, is sharp, distinct. "A British wine, if you please. Perhaps from the vineyards of Castel Coch. If you have some."

I know where the wine is, but am less sure of his intentions.

Is he who I think he is? This is the first time one has been in my shop, and the thought repulses me, but if it might assist in leading me to Amanda then surely the risk is worth taking.

I cough to clear my throat, regain some composure. "Those wines can be rather expensive."

I feel him bristling with anger, then reduce it; calm down; as I knew he would.

"Do you not think I can pay?"

"You can have two bottles for nothing," I say, "in exchange for some information."

He laughs. The sound is eerie, not in the slightest bit amusing. When I return his laugh, my own is hollow.

"And what kind of information would a shopkeeper like yourself be looking for?"

I pause. Then take the risk and turn around, reach up for the two bottles, leaving myself completely unprotected should he wish to strike. I hope my bravery will impress him, or, at the very least, intrigue him.

I place the bottles on the counter, keep both of my hands tight around their necks. "I'm looking for a girl."

When he smiles this time I can see the tip of his elongated incisors, gleaming white. "Shopkeeper, I am not in the profession of running a brothel. And the girls that I keep acquaintance with would not be to your taste."

"Not just any girl," I say. "A specific girl."

He shakes his head. "I will choose to pay in the usual currency rather than give you such information." He reaches out a smooth white hand, which, under the lantern light might have been bone itself. "Now give me the wine . . . "

145

"Wait . . ."

But I am too late. In an instant coins are clattering on the table top, and the bottles have left my hands, my palms sting with the speed at which they have been taken, the shop door open with its bell ringing madly as though a Peeler's whistle. Gone. Already he has gone.

*

It was my sister who had brought Amanda into womanhood. Suffering a facial disfigurement caused by a swinging Tube train door, she was destined never to marry and for a while she lived with me; tending to Amanda during the day, and berating me with her tongue during the evening hours. She never had a good word to say about me, which I attributed to a sibling jealousy of my own looks and business stature; but I couldn't ask her to leave as Amanda would have left with her.

Despite the ill will I felt towards my daughter at her birth and for several years after, I couldn't deny that she was my flesh and blood. And more importantly, the only flesh and blood I would ever have.

When my sister died of the plague it was I who burnt her body. I won't lie and say that it gave me no pleasure to do so. By that time Amanda was almost a grown woman, fourteen and fully budded. And despite her sex she had taken a great interest in the wines. I pinned my hopes on her, and for that maybe I was just another fool.

Whenever I was sick, Amanda saw to the shop. She became a favourite with my customers, brightening up the place

146

with her laughter and her knowledge. Under her guidance we added other products, cheeses that might complement the wine, and glasses into which they might be poured. She had a wider vision, there was no doubt about that, and soon enough she had her share of suitors.

Of course, being her father this sat uneasily with me, as doubtless such things have with every daughter's father that came before me and likely all those that will go after. Not simply in terms of honour, but for what would happen to the shop should she ever leave.

London was a sprawling metropolis, larger—we were told —than Rome had ever been. It bustled with myriad people, was filled with new technological advances, and was naturally at the hub of my world. Yet, within this seething morass of culture, this shop —my business—retained its identity as the finest purveyor of wines. Orders flooded in from all corners of the capital. With only Amanda to help me—God forbid I would allow another man's *child* to interfere in my business—what would I do if she were to go? So I put my thumb down on many of her suitors, without realising as I did so that it just drove them underground.

*

I take my cloak from the hanger and slip it over my shoulders. I lock the front door and place the key in my pocket, then turn out the lantern and enter the backroom. Amanda should be sitting by the fire, going through the accounts, and her absence creates a vacuum in my heart. Will I ever again watch her features as they are illuminated by firelight, without an accompanying fear that they would turn to dust in daylight? But I can't sit here waiting to be told the answer to that question, and as usual there is nothing for it but to go and look for her.

I leave by the back entrance, pull my cloak tightly around me. Push my hat down over my forehead so that almost all that can be seen are my eyes and slanted nose. London has regained some of its night-time passion over the past few years. When they first arrived, there was panic, confusion, sheer terror. Now there sits an uneasy truce, even attempts to enter Parliament! Their red insignia is a stand, they say, against whomsoever it was that first cursed them. But no one is sufficiently convinced by these political arguments to accept them. No one, that is, except the young.

I take a right through the alley and enter the street that runs across the front of the shop, glance up at the painted sign that announces: *John Bamford, Purveyor of Fine Wines*; and remember first my disappointment that it would never read *John Bamford & Son*, and secondly my lack of courage to make it *John Bamford & Daughter*. It wasn't as if I didn't acknowledge her. I treated her as an equal. She had nothing to rebel against, yet this had come to pass.

I bite down on my lip, push myself forwards, try to convince myself that all is not yet lost.

I stop at my usual haunt, The Slaughtered Lamb on Landis Avenue. George fetches me a tankard of ale and we have our usual argument about alcohol that always ends in agreement. He is the only one I have told about Amanda's absence; if the others are aware of it then they have had the courtesy to stay quiet.

"Any news?" he asks, when our banter about wines and ales has run its course.

I shake my head, then tell him about the last customer of

148

the day.

"They're getting bold," he says. "Don't underestimate their political weight. The Ministers aren't daft, they'll use them to their advantage; there was even talk the other day that they'd make good Peelers."

My body shakes at the thought. "You're not serious?"

"Why not, John? They have the height. They command the terror if not the respect. And should they agree—as has been mooted—to feed only on the criminals, then what's to stop them taking on the role of law enforcement?"

"Common decency?" I mutter, almost under my breath but not quite. "How can we trust them?"

"Ah, now there lies the secret of their success," George nods, pouring me another ale. "We can't."

*

The night plods on. I venture further than my local, to places I wouldn't ordinarily go. Here, amongst strangers, I feel that I might be able to show my photograph of Amanda without fear of arousing suspicion as to who she was; thus avoiding some kind of retribution. Families have been driven to the outskirts of the capital once it is known that their relatives have turned. Instead, I make suggestions that she was no more than a runaway, no doubt prostituting herself on the streets after a silly family argument. To elicit sympathy, I say my wife is out of her mind with worry.

Most people I approach shake their heads. More than a few hold onto the photo for longer than is necessary, but I withhold the urge to pummel their lascivious faces with my fists. Several times I

149

skirt the entrance to the Underground tunnels, knowing that my answers might be found within, but too scared to enter there with the equal knowledge that I might well never return. Just as I hope and pray Amanda is simply walking a thin line between light and dark, I also tread that same line between red and white.

I remember clearly when her interest was piqued. Too young to appreciate the fear that first came from the plague and then the vampires, her reaction to the official announcement of their existence was the same that one might attribute to a new invention. Something which one might visit at the Crystal Palace and gasp with wonder at its intricacies, whilst at the same time knowing next to nothing about how it worked. I could see her intrigue bubbling there, but never sought to deflect it. I thought talking about matters openly might more likely negate the myth.

If there were warning signs then I disregarded them, but even I couldn't fail to see the attraction these monstrous beings held for the general public. The newspapers were full of such things; Amanda's hands were blackened by the print. But are conditions truly so bad for some of the lower classes that they would voluntarily join the undead to improve their lot? Are there really secret societies amongst the higher classes where vampires and Lords mix cocktails, and talk politics; later indulging in such orgies that would put the Hellfire Club to shame? Speculation is rife, facts are few; no one seems to differentiate between the two.

One night, Amanda put her accounts to one side, stood up, and went towards the window where the darkness fell softly against the pane, only our fire keeping it from the room.

"I want to go out," she said.

I ask you, what kind of father could possibly acquiesce to

such a request?

*

Now I find myself amongst the prostitutes of Whitechapel, who stand in twos and threes, afraid to move out of their little groups for whatever reason might scare them. I show the photograph guardedly. Few of them have even seen a photograph before, and it's all I have of Amanda to keep her in my memory. I don't get much response, and only a handful of inappropriate offers that I'm too tired and much to focussed to take seriously.

Around the corner from here, as I well know, the Fabian Society is no doubt debating the morality of the vampire. Wells, Bernard Shaw, the sexologist Havelock Ellis. Don't they realise that some kind of acceptance of vampire lore is tantamount to accepting them into our homes? Once I heard as a fact that a vampire might only cross a threshold if it had been invited, but now it's become a myth as its authenticity has been eroded. Does knowledge beget knowledge, or does it, in fact, create knowledge? All I know is that a vampire entered my shop today and left with two bottles of wine.

I glance up at the lit windows. Emmeline Pankhurst might well be in there. And how much might she also be culpable in Amanda's curiosity and disobedience? The Woman's Franchise League was unnecessarily empowering women. Christ knows that my relationship with my own daughter is forward-thinking and not backward. The perpetuity of my own business depends upon it. But what Pankhurst is doing is simply opening a can of worms. Freethinking has lent my daughter a political mind. And from that

151

has created interest in the disenfranchised.

I spit on the street outside their door and move on quickly.

The night seems blacker now than it has ever been, although I know this to be my imagination. Is it the possibility of my daughter's death that has drawn a veil across my world, or is it the fear that she might be alive but not alive? Again, actual hard facts about the vampires' habits are hard to find within the city. No one trusts the newspapers to know the truth, yet everyone has a different answer. Is the Blood Cell part of that myth, or does it really exist? As I continue to walk I push such things out of my mind, try to remember my daughter whilst I still have a mind to think with.

It is true that I had only begun to notice her since my sister's death. During the daylight hours I had toiled in the shop, heard only occasional squeals of play behind the door that led to my back room; and even more occasionally my sister admonishing her for some misdeed. Invariably she loved the child, who had almost been my gift to her, and at the time I didn't resent their play or their companionship. But now . . . if things had been different? Would I have spent more time with Amanda as a child? Would it have made a difference as to how much time I would spend with her as an adult?

The questions foam as thick in my brain as did the head on George's ales. As I turn yet another corner I am so consumed by my thoughts that I don't see the gentleman until I am already on top of him.

Quick as the one who had left my shop earlier that day, I am lifted off the ground and held up against the wall by my throat. My feet kicking at air beneath me, my nostrils clamouring to be away from the stench. Raised from the ground as I was, we were at the same height. His breath rancid, his teeth an abomination. Yet I withhold the urge to spit in his face as I had done the doorway, and instead I meet his gaze as his anger cools and he lets me down.

"My apologies," I splutter, as my breath returns to me.

He begins to walk away.

"Wait."

He turns. A look of dreadful curiosity on his face. I doubt whether anyone has ever told him to wait before. I have to speak quickly, to outrun his impatience.

"I'm looking for my daughter. She may have joined the Blood Cell either willingly or as a victim. I suspect the former, but either way I need to speak to her. I need to know."

He looks the way a dog might look, quizzical but not particularly bothered.

"This should concern me?"

"Please," I say; then I notice he is wearing a wedding ring on his finger. "If you ever had a child yourself, then you will know."

He had followed my gaze. God knows what kind of memories these creatures hold, but I knew he had to have been something once, before he had become what he became. A certain trigger pulls taut within him, although I wouldn't speculate that it was compassion.

"This daughter of yours. What does she look like?"

I remove the photograph from my breast pocket with trembling hands. He takes it from me as someone might pick a playing card. Uncertain as to whether he was being tricked.

Then he flicks it back at me, the corner nicking my face,

153

drawing blood.

I put up a hand to defend myself, but he is already upon me; knocking me to the floor. His tongue grazing the length of my cheek.

"Don't be concerned," he whispers, as I fight my rising gorge, "no one ever died from a lick."

I close my eyes tight. Pray.

When I open them he is standing above me. "I know her," he says. "When I last saw her she was still human. She was assisting us in our political campaign. Look for Goulston Street."

"Goulston Street? But that's . . . "

Too late. Already he is gone.

*

The night isn't over yet. I get to my feet and stagger over to the wall, feel my face. The blood in my wound has coagulated, but I don't know whether this is a good sign. I bend down and retch, bring up the ale and the remnants of my lunch. I feel no different, and after a few moments I realise I haven't been turned. For whatever reason, for the moment I have been spared.

Goulston Street isn't far from where I am. It is infamous, of course. The Ripper had reportedly left a message chalked on the wall there, but whether that holds any significance to my personal quest I don't stop to think. Instead, I search the dark ground for the photograph of Amanda and soon find it, thankfully intact. I tuck it back into my pocket, then go on my way.

I remember a quote I had read, attributed to the poet John Dryden: *Death in itself is nothing; but we fear to be we know not what, we*

154

know not where. And as I walk I wonder what I might fear the most, losing Amanda or losing myself.

I come upon Goulston Street easily enough. It is not deserted, as I expected, but filled with an angry mob, some of them bearing lighted torches. Many of them with makeshift weapons. A few of them with guns. It seems I wasn't the only one looking for something this night. The city has been polarised, no doubt by ale and outrage, the usual proponents of unthinking behaviour. On another night I might happily have joined them, but looking up at one of the windows of the wooden tenement building, I think I catch a glimpse of raven-black hair and a familiar face.

"Amanda!"

My shout is lost in the crowd, which even now pushes forwards, dragging me with it as I stumble and try to regain my balance. I look at the faces of the men alongside me; wretched every one of them. Nothing to lose, but perhaps a bit of fame to gain. It is impossible to fight against the mob, so I turn with them and begin to force my way into the building, into the front; hoping I might reach Amanda before the rest of them are able.

I can see in their eyes that they would make no distinction between vampire and political assistant. What tarred one, would surely tar the other.

And as I carry myself forward I pray to the God that I have always believed in. Not the one that had killed my wife and son, nor the one that is worshipped in the churches. But the little one that lives inside of me, the one that I can talk to through the bad times even though I might neglect him during the good. The one who has given me the strength to search for Amanda, when

155

a lesser man with a lesser God might have given up.

We climb the stairs. At the top is a corridor with several doors to the left and right. If my bearings are correct then Amanda must be in the room nearest to my right, facing the street, maybe deliberating whether to jump. The door is wooden and locked. An axe is thrust into my hands, and I use it aware of the irony that I might be letting her murderers into the room as I am trying to save her. I don't dare call her name aloud, but repeat it constantly in my head.

And then we are through, spilling into the room. Which is empty.

A few sticks of furniture, some papers, little else. And then the noise starts. A horrific, grinding noise that sends cries of terror amongst the men. I run to the window and look outside. The building is being vacated, fast. Yet outside of it the vampires are feasting, maybe as they have never done so before. In front of the entire mob, whose attempted blows are met with speed and laughter. Who are being cut down and turned into ribbons.

I look up, away from the scene. Look out over a London that stretches as far as the eye can see. How long would it take them to take this city? They don't need the political campaign. It is breathtaking. The city is here, right in their grasp, in all its magnificence. They only need the numbers. They need recruits.

Someone shoots me in the back.

As I fall I turn to see the man who had fired. I see from his face that he realises his mistake. And then he is off. I close my eyes.

Pain spreads out across my lower back like a bloodstain. Maybe this is how she knows I am there.

When I open my eyes again I see Amanda bending over me. She is spotless, smooth, either herself or a good imitation. I can't quite work out what the look means in her eyes, but at the moment of my death I know I don't want to die.

Her lips part, and I beg the God inside me that I might see that she has fangs.

So that she might save me.

Or damn me.

Or both.

Up

It's said that anyone can remember what they were doing when Kennedy was shot, or when Thatcher stepped down, or when they heard about 9/11. Added to that I'm sure we'll know where we were that day when everyone went up. Assuming, that is, people will be left to tell the tale.

I was nineteen when it happened. I hadn't been watching the news because I'd spent the entire weekend in a drunken haze with a new boyfriend who became an old boyfriend immediately afterwards. I left his house that morning still overhung, not really registering that there were more people than usual on the streets for that time of day. Nor that they were all looking up. It was cold. A crisp Autumn start. The pavements were slippery with a thin patina of frost, the skies blue and cloudless. It could have been just like any other day. A day where nothing unusual would happen.

Then I heard a shout and watched as the door to a terraced house opened across the street. The occupant, an old woman who looked to be in her eighties, was wailing and crying for help. On an ordinary day, of course, she wouldn't have got a reaction. People would have walked by, on their way to work, on their way to anywhere else where they didn't have to deal with someone's grief. So that's why I stopped and stared when half a dozen members of the public entered her house, one of them consoling her on her steps; all with expectation on their faces that seemed way beyond commonsense.

I lit a cigarette and inhaled the smoke, wondering why I did it and why it seemed purer than the air. I leant against an oak tree and watched as more people were attracted to the house like iron filings to a magnet. There was a compulsion, almost a reverence to their movements that was beyond me. And then the door opened again and a body was dragged down the steps. The wailing woman reached out for it as it passed her and I realised it must have been her husband. I started to walk towards the group myself, wanting to get a better look, car-crash fascination after all. They stood around the body, three deep by now, I was so transfixed that I forgot to put out my cigarette; it burnt illegally within my fingers as I stood within ten feet of possible non-smokers. Then, just as I could see properly, those who held the body let it go and it rose into the air like my toxic smoke, floated slowly upwards, far into the sky, until we could no longer see anything other than a dot that eventually disappeared into infinity.

I called Rosie on my Blackberry. *You'll never believe what I've just seen.*

Where've you been? I've been trying to contact you all weekend!

Long story.

Come on over, there's so much to tell you. Craig was one of the floaters.

I didn't ask her what she meant, because somehow I

already knew. Eventually, the term *floater* became replaced by *the risen*.

*

Rosie lived in Suffolk Square, a concrete block tenement building on the other side of town. I decided to walk it. The buses were unreliable, dangerous, and crowded. I lit another cigarette despite my asthma, and tried to keep my breathing steady. Jasper, the guy I'd spent the weekend with, was already bleeding out of my mind and became replaced by memories of Craig. My ex of two years. Rosie had taken up with him since, and had had as bad a time as I did. As a drug user, thief, and would-be pimp, he didn't have a lot going for him. But between us we'd tried to keep him on the straight and narrow, however futile it proved to be.

Rosie was a non-smoker but she didn't stick by the rules when it came to me. She opened the door to her flat and I realised she'd been crying. Blackness pooled beneath her eyes from her mascara and lack of sleep. Nu-Retro-Metal blasted out of her music player, louder than the bangs on the walls of the neighbours next door. Even *I* had to ask her to turn it down as I entered her flat. I couldn't hear her and I couldn't hear myself think.

We sat on her pale yellow sofa and she handed me a beer. I fizzed it open, but didn't drink. It wasn't too early in the morning, but I needed to calm down. I'd been shaking since Rosie had mentioned Craig and a beer wouldn't help. Rosie looked at me quizzically then went to make a cup of tea. I watched as she boiled the kettle and poured hot water over the

160

tea bag. When she stirred it I noticed she was shaking too.

"Where have you been?" she asked, as she sat down again.

"With some guy, it's not important. Tell me about Craig."

"I didn't see it, but I heard about it. He was with some of his druggie mates in the park. This was late Friday night. Anyway, something happened. Either he O'D or was stabbed—no one seems to know—but after he died his body started to float upwards. The rest of them just watched, then one of them phoned me. I thought they were off their heads until I saw what was happening on the news."

"I saw something myself," I said. "This morning. An old man floated into the sky."

"It's everywhere," Rosie said. "This is worldwide. Haven't you seen the news at all?"

I shook my head and she turned on the television. She flicked through the channels quickly, all of them carrying reports about the same thing. We watched as bodies rose upwards in a stately fashion. We were transfixed, fused with a sense of awe and fear. After a while I realised the same reports were on a loop. Maybe the incidents were isolated after all.

"Where are they going?" I asked.

"According to the news they don't know. Once they hit our atmosphere they seem to disappear."

"Are they souls?"

Rosie shrugged. "Who knows? It's only the recently dead, or so they think."

My mind wandered as I imagined bodies rising and hitting the wood of their coffins, remaining suspended in the air without anyone knowing. I shivered. It creeped me out.

"I'm sorry about Craig," I said.

"He had it coming to him. We both know that."

Then Rosie leant into me, and I rested her head on my shoulder and stroked her hair as she sobbed her tiny broken heart out.

*

When I returned to my flat it looked tired and empty, much like myself. Detritus was everywhere. Rubbish on the floor by the sofa, in the kitchen, cigarette stubs and used condoms in the bedroom. I wished it were *that* junk which floated up into the sky instead of dead people, although I guess we'd pumped enough crap into the atmosphere already. Maybe that was the cause of the floaters—I preferred to call them that, like making a joke to pretend everything was all right—maybe the atmosphere was absorbing us into it and saying *here, see how you like it.*

No scientific explanations had been proffered for the phenomenon, although there were plenty of religious ones. No particular faith had been affected, the floating was indiscriminate of persuasion. Of course, the churches, mosques, synagogues were all full. If I had been a believer I'd have considered attending. Instead I lay on my back on my bed, my head turned to the window to see whether anyone would float by. Eventually, I fell asleep.

When I awoke my face was pushed against the ceiling. I yelled and waved my arms underneath me. It was the dream of falling, that sinking feeling just before waking, the sudden drop.

But it wasn't a dream, just blind panic as I flapped and twisted and turned, bobbing on the air as though afloat on an invisible sea.

It took me awhile to stop fighting. When I did I managed to turn myself over and look downwards. A smidgeon of comfort assuaged me as I didn't see myself dead on the bed. Wasn't that what happened in out of body experiences? Or was that simply the filmic version? Then I remembered that the news had mentioned no residue when bodies had left the ground, so maybe that meant I *was* dead after all? My wet tears fell to the floor, they didn't rise.

I remained hovering for several minutes, gradually coming to terms with what was happening. I was certain I was alive, I'd seen plenty of dead people to be sure of that, so why was I afloat? I bent my body downwards and kicked against the ceiling, propelling myself towards the window where I could grab hold of the curtain rail. Outside it was deserted, hardly anybody in sight. But those I could see were clinging onto objects - park benches, lampposts, branches. One woman was suspended in the air, clenching the lead that anchored her to a dog that was barking at her from the ground. It made me glad that I was indoors.

I wondered how long I'd been asleep. It looked like mid-afternoon, the sun was already low in the sky and the ascending bodies took on a romantic pinkish hue. Of course, these weren't rising as steadily as the dead, many were flapping their arms—in fright not in flight—and some were screaming. But they couldn't manoeuvre themselves back to the earth, it was as though gravity's hold had been lifted.

My arms began to ache as I gripped the curtain rail. If

163

there were blue sky above me then how long would I be able to hold on before it took me? Would I feel scared or exhilarated? Would it be the beginning of the end?

My mobile rang. I managed to wriggle it out of my pocket one handed whilst keeping my grip firm on the rail. Then I decided just to let go, to regain my strength, and bobbed back to the ceiling where I took the call. It was Rosie. No surprises there.

"Are you okay?" Her voice was trembling, I could guess why.

"Of sorts," I said.

"Have you been watching the news?"

"I've been asleep, but I *have* looked out the window."

"It's not just the dead any more," Rosie said. "The living have started to rise."

"Tell me about it."

"You?"

"Yes. You?"

"No."

"Well, that makes me feel special then."

Rosie paused. I had a feeling she was scared of asking the next question, wary if she wanted to know the answer.

"Where are you now?"

"I'm on my ceiling. Want to come over and pull me down?"

I could almost hear her thinking about it. Then very faintly she said *yes*. Again, I knew why she had to consider it. Coming over to mine would involve being outside and if she took off there would be nothing to anchor her. I almost cried again in the knowledge that she was prepared to risk it for me.

164

We were good friends, but I wasn't sure if I would have risked it for her.

Whilst waiting for her I attempted some tricks. Pushing myself off the ceiling I found I could do a somersault, like astronauts in space. Sure I was ungainly, hitting my back and face roughly against the Artex, but it was a gentle force that exerted itself upon me. I wasn't literally rocketing upwards. But any pleasure was tainted by considering my future. Was I to spend the rest of my life like this, indoors? How would I eat? How would I get to the toilet?

When Rosie arrived she stood open mouthed for a while, before standing on my bed and pulling me downwards. We hugged. She said afterwards that she could feel her feet lifting as she held onto me, as though I were a buoyancy aid. The journey over had been quiet, she'd had to walk it. There was a constant fear that she would rise off the pavement.

She took my hand and led me into the living room and switched on the television. Reports were wild now, full of speculation. At a rough estimate 1.2 billion had been affected. Many were like myself: stuck indoors. The rest were lost to the skies.

"They still don't know where they're going," Rosie said. "It's unclear whether they disintegrate when they leave the Earth's atmosphere or whether it's more magical than that. How do you feel?"

"Light-headed," I joked. But in some ways it was true. I had begun to feel free, as though I were leaving my worldly worries behind as well as the world itself.

"Why me?" I said. Then I asked Rosie to fetch a cigarette. Again, she wasn't bothered that I was floating within ten feet of her. We both knew the current laws were ridiculous.

"You know what will happen," said Rosie. "This really is the end of the world as we know it."

"I feel fine," I joked.

"Seriously. We'll be entering a new dark age. You remember that stuff at school about the Middle Ages?"

I nodded. I recalled the first series of *Blackadder* and Polanski's *Macbeth*. Our school had been quite liberal when it came to learning aids.

"Eventually there won't be enough people to make power. There won't be televisions. There won't be the Internet. People will have to think for themselves again. In some of the poorer countries looting has already started—at least, from those who're not too scared to go out."

"Maybe it won't stop there," I said. "Maybe we'll all start to rise."

"Maybe," Rosie said.

*

Once night fell we turned off the television. Rosie still hadn't floated, so I let her take my bed whilst I hung over her like a vampire. There was no noise at all from outside. I had learnt enough now to move from room to room, gaining views of two sides of the street. Anyone who had been outside when they left the ground had now left the planet. Everyone else was inside—floating or not. It wasn't difficult to see how swiftly the world would decline. What if no one went to work tomorrow, or the day after that? How long could we survive without being able to shop?

Then I remembered the woman and her dog. We had watched as the dog had become accustomed to his mistress hovering over him, and before sunset he had led her back to their home. She had managed to get close enough to the ground to open her front door and I imagined her relief as they entered the building. They lived in a flat right across the street from me, and I watched as she bobbed up to her ceiling and looked out to me across the divide. The first thing she did was light a cigarette. I would have done the same thing. And I did.

I realised how light she must have been for the dog to lead her. Rosie also didn't seem to have any problems with me. I thought about my life to date, about how I had progressed from one failed relationship to another. About how I'd never held down a job. About how I probably would never hold down a job. What did my future hold for me? Wouldn't it be better to soar during my final days? Maybe we were being beamed up by an alien civilisation to lead a better life. Maybe it wasn't the catastrophe that we were led to believe?

I closed my eyes and slept. Perhaps unsurprisingly my dreams were of flying. I was passing over new lands, new places that I hadn't seen before. Deserts, fields, fjords, cities, mountains, seas. I saw no one else during my flight. No one even in the skies. When I awoke it was with a jolt, but I hadn't fallen. I was still over the bed and Rosie was looking out of the window.

"I want to go out," I said. There was no question about it. I had to get outside and into the air.

Rosie looked at me, horrified.

"Don't worry," I said, "I have some rope."

She didn't argue. She fetched it and tied it tightly around my waist. Then led me outside as though I were a helium balloon. I bobbed above her at an even pace. Whilst the rope tugged against my middle there was no danger of rising. I found I wasn't even worried about her letting go. That wasn't the case with Rosie. Her fingers were white from the tightness of her grip.

We walked over to the park, the same park where Craig had left this mortal coil. I felt guilty for Rosie, losing her man and her best friend over the course of two days, but I made a decision and slipped the knife out of my pocket. I held it close to the rope. Then I closed my eyes and thought of cutting through.

"You know I have a theory," Rosie said, keeping her eyes to the ground, fearful of tripping and letting me go. "I haven't seen it on the news, but everyone I know who has floated has been a smoker, and those I know who haven't floated, aren't."

"That's a bit silly," I said. I looked up at the inviting sky, so open and welcoming. Then I cut through the rope with the knife.

Rosie gasped. I shouted *sorry*, and let the knife drop so she would know that it wasn't her fault. Then I looked away, I didn't want to watch her watching me. I needed to bask in the moment of my ascension, my awakening. The sheer sense of self that was embedded in my actions. The ground fell away from me slowly, as though I were growing larger and larger, filling up with the exhilaration of existence. And then when the land became uniform, nothing discernible beneath me, my perspective altered and I was shrinking, shrinking, lost in the vastness of the sky.

I was high, very high, when others began to hurtle passed me on their way down.

I watched them go, as flailing bodies became pinpricks then red dots on the earth. But my euphoria remained, being *up* was upbeat. I was on a cigarette high.

After a while I eased out my Blackberry and recorded my story—I had to do something with my life after all.

So if this has survived as a record after the fall then maybe, just maybe, I did too.

Shipping Tomorrow Backwards

Millie knew exactly when the voice entered her head. It was a bright spring morning. The 8th April 2004. She was washing up the breakfast things—a plate for her toast and a mug of half-drunk tea —just as she always did immediately after breakfast, even though it had been a while since she'd had to look after anyone other than herself. Standards were standards after all.

Through the window of her cottage she could see a male blackbird pulling at something in the grass. Obviously a worm. Sunlight glinted off the water in the lily pad-shaped stone birdbath. Buds were pushing their way through the extremities of trees, and up through the dark soil. It had rained overnight. She could smell the difference in the air. It was fresh.

It was then, suddenly, without warning: Clive's voice in her ear. *I love you.*

She dropped the mug she was washing back into the bowl where the cushion of water couldn't prevent it from cracking the submerged plate. Suds flew up like cotton-wool moths. Slowly, she looked around.

Empty, of course; the room was as empty as it had to be. Clive was long dead.

She listened again, intently, but nothing came. Her old, wrinkled fingers gripped the edge of the plastic washing-up bowl. It had been a young voice. She felt numb.

*

Millie and Clive had met shortly after the end of the Second World War. As was typical in those euphoric times, they fell in love swiftly. Perhaps on reflection they were both simply glad to be alive. Clive had flown planes, made bombing raids over Germany, and returned safely each time even when over half of his comrades had died. Millie had worked in a munitions factory, making bombs she knew would kill people. But the atmosphere in the factory was always upbeat. They were on the right side; they were on the winning side. They had to believe it because it was all that they had.

In December 1945 she had caught Clive's eye outside the Regal. *The Lost Weekend* had been showing, with Ray Milland and Jane Wyman. None of her friends had particularly liked it. It wasn't really the kind of movie they wanted to see, but they saw it anyway because it was good just to be able to see something. She was with a group of five girls from the factory and he was with four of his mates. She often wondered what happened to the odd girl out. The rest of them had paired up that evening, and Irene and Frank had also got married, just like her and Clive, less than five months later.

*

171

It wasn't until the following summer that she heard it again. Tuesday evening. 10th August. *Coronation Street* on the telly, with the sound turned loud because of her failing hearing. There was an argument brewing between Ken and Mike—she'd lived through so many of them. Then, there it was again: *I love you.* In her ear. Quite clearly.

She looked around quickly this time, but of course he wasn't there. Was it a ghost? Surely not. He hadn't believed in such things, and neither did she. It was a young voice, not the rasp that his had become when he died; his trip to the heavens fuelled by years of cigarettes and coal dust. Three years ago now, and she in her eighties herself. *How long?* She thought. *How much longer for her?*

After *Coronation Street* was over she switched off the television and walked slowly around the cottage, touching things. The tea towel hanging on the sucker pad adjacent to the sink. The one they'd bought in Dorset on their last holiday together: Weymouth, Poole, Corfe Castle, Swanage, and other places printed upon its now faded, almost grubby surface. The straw-made donkey from Benidorm—they knew it was tat when they bought it, but it still had a place here in this house. The edges of the straw scraping her fingers as she ran them over the object. On the sideboard, the two Swiss-house viewfinders, which flicked over alpine scenes when you pressed down the chimney and looked through the windows. These were their mementos, and, in a way, they were amongst the only links that led to Clive after his death. Unlike her memory, which she thought could do nothing but fade, however she tried to stop it.

172

*

They began married life in a terraced house. Council owned of course. She considered herself lucky. Clive was always considerate, never complained. Not like the men she'd heard from stories told by other women in her street. He wasn't always down the pub either. After work he'd head straight to the table, eat the food she'd prepared for him, and after watching the news on the small black and white television they'd saved up for, they'd head for bed. She was barren, but Clive didn't seem to mind. They had each other, he said. What more could they want?

*

It took a while for her to tell anyone. She knew it wasn't her imagination. She wasn't going mad or—god forbid—senile. She didn't leave the gas on whilst she was cooking, or forget to feed the cat, or find herself wandering around the high street without knowing why she was there or where she was going.

Every Thursday she'd get her free lunch provided for by the community church even though she was hardly a regular at their services. Betty said she should come more often, but she wanted the company of friends and not that of a god. Everyone seemed to have forgotten the privations of the war. How could you slip back into worshipping a benefactor who had allowed the killings of so many people? She never bought the idea that prayer had won them the war. Blood and guts had done that.

She exercised daily. Nothing too frenetic, just some tips she'd followed on GMTV. Keeping the blood flowing through her

173

veins, keeping her muscles active. She prided herself on her health, as Clive had done before he died. Except for the stuff in his lungs which he knew could never be removed. So she was well aware of her mental and physical capabilities. She had friends, didn't talk to herself. Just had someone talking to her.

I love you.

It became regular. Not so regular that you could set your watch by it, not like the real Clive who was such a stickler for routine, but more like her: spontaneous, impulsive. Several times a day, in her ear: *I love you.*

One morning, she went to her doctors. Chose her words carefully.

"This voice," he said. "Where do you hear it?"

"In my ear," she answered. "As though he were there. It's not in my head. It feels outside of it."

He smiled, but she didn't feel reassured.

"Has it a pattern?"

"It's identical," she said. "Whenever I hear it. The tone, the nuance, the words. The same."

"It's a memory," he said.

She nodded. She knew.

*

When had he first spoken those words? Perhaps a week or so after they had met at the pictures, perhaps later. How many times had he spoken those words? Daily, weekly? She couldn't be sure. They had become such a part of her life that she couldn't imagine life without them, just as she couldn't imagine life without Clive.

174

It was like driving and accidentally slipping into reverse. Not just hearing those words, but everything else. The anomalies when they'd been together when it had been two steps forward and one step back. Like shipping tomorrow backwards, he had put it. Such an easy way with words, with excuses. It hadn't always been perfect.

The first time he had done it she ignored it. The second time she tried to ignore it. The third time he promised it was the last time and she believed him and was proven right.

I love you.

The voice was young. When had he said those words—those precise words—exactly?

*

The doctor explained that he thought she may have had a stroke. It had been mild, which was why she hadn't noticed it. He called it a transient ischemic attack. He asked her to lift her arms over her head and watched to see how long she could hold them up. He asked her to smile. He asked her to repeat *the quick brown fox jumped over the lazy dog*. He touched the sides of her face.

Then he explained that a mini-stroke is caused by minor blockages in brain arteries, as well as some other things that she found she wasn't interested in understanding. She knew that she was okay, she had been for several months if the diagnosis was correct. She didn't need to know exactly what the symptoms or diagnosis might be. She just needed to know about the voice.

He sent her to a neurologist.

In the meantime she'd figured it out for herself, and the

175

neurologist only added fancy words to her own prognosis. He told her of a famous case of a woman of similar age who had begun to hear Irish music amid background chatter which turned out to be the memories of her upbringing as a five year old. Memories which she'd no longer had in any form since the family had moved to America. Memories that were unbidden—that had no reason to surface other than because of a random stimulation—memories that she cherished.

"If it troubles you," he said, "we can give you a drug."

*

Back in her home Millie thought long and hard. She had known it was a memory, albeit the strongest, most succinct and perfectly formed memory that she had ever had, yet she felt deflated that the diagnosis had agreed with her. It closed a door somewhere deep within her body. And when another door opened, it let in some rain.

She lay in bed. Her cat, a tortoiseshell by the name of Sukie, sat on her stomach, looking directly into her eyes. She looked back. There was life there, but not the same life as hers. There was intelligence, but not the same intelligence. Yet it was looking at her, it was choosing to look at her. There was some reason behind its actions. But she didn't choose the memory and it didn't choose her. It existed through a tripped synapse somewhere in her brain. Other than being a pure memory, it was meaningless.

Did she really want to hear those words, over and over again, until she died? Would their repetition replace the other memories of Clive? Would all her memories of him be reduced to those three little words? Indiscriminately?

*

"I love you."

She turned her back on him.

He grabbed her by the shoulders and she could feel the need.

"Didn't you hear me, I said *I love you*."

"I hear you clearly enough." She turned to face him. Found the strength. "And so did she, I expect. Did you say the same thing to her?"

He stammered. Wouldn't look her in the eye. She held his gaze as it darted about like a hummingbird.

"Did you?"

He shook his head, but it was really a nod.

"It wasn't the same," he pleaded. "I didn't mean it."

"You meant it sure enough," she said.

She went to get the pills.

The Glass Football

I don't think we ever meant to kick her. It was just something that happened. One of those things that you tend to slide into when you're at school. One moment you're in the right group, then you're in the wrong group. Then someone's down on the floor and there's a boot going in. It was just that one time it happened to be a girl. Whether she went down by mistake, or we pushed her, or whatever; there she was and my right boot was heading towards her face. Amazingly, no one grassed. I'd probably forgotten about it by the end of the week. No doubt it took Melanie longer, but surely she would have done so eventually.

*

Dermot never entered rooms, he bled into them. One moment he wouldn't be there, and then, slowly, like watching the minute hand on a clock, he would be. You could only track his presence by comparing where he was to where he had been.

    If this sounds confusing, then that's because it is. Dermot

was someone short of an identity. He had no presence until he segued into that of others. He was the pause between one song finishing and the other song starting. I always wondered why he came to parties at all.

Emma had the same opinion, except with one major difference. She fancied him.

There was a student party in a small terrace off Unthank Road that we gate-crashed one evening, Emma and I on our way back from The Lily Langtry after a night of friendly drinks. The front door was partly open, and Emma seemed to think that she knew who lived there, but as it turned out she didn't, although that was of no consequence. A Nouvelle Vague CD was winding down the evening, their version of 'Dancing With Myself' playing as we entered the room. At first we couldn't see anyone we know, but after a while we spotted Dermot in the corner of the room. He was smoking, looking bored, talking to no one.

We'd managed to find ourselves a place on a tattered sofa that had accumulated wine stains in a Rorschach test pattern. It sank in the middle, so we were squashed together shoulder to shoulder and we weren't going to move. Someone lent us a corkscrew for the bottle of red we'd bought from the off-licence after leaving the pub, and we took turns swigging from it. A couple of girls were in the centre of the room, dancing to the music, their skirts swirling around the tops of their knees. Emma nudged my elbow. I thought she'd noticed I was watching them, but instead she nodded across to Dermot. He'd finished his cigarette, but its absence was the only indication that he'd moved.

I fancied Emma something rotten, of course. I think she knew it, but we went under the pretence of only being friends.

179

Another night she'd told me Dermot attracted her, but I was sober then. Now I said: "What do you see in him, anyway?"

"Nothing," she said. "Which is exactly why I like him."

I'd always found Dermot hard to describe and Emma's opinion didn't add much either. Sometimes I'd say that I could describe him only by discounting what he wasn't. Once you'd gone through all the physical, emotional, spiritual elements you could think of, then what was left would be Dermot. No one I ever knew had managed to have a deep conversation with him. He was as shallow as the reflection of a ghost.

And yet, unlike even a ghost, he was always there. Always invited, always in the newsagents when you popped in for the packet of fags you'd promised to give up, always at your shoulder in the pub just before buying a round. He was like a visible invisible man.

He wasn't just simply tolerated. Sometimes I thought it might only be me - that I singled him out because I knew Emma had a thing for him and it annoyed me - but once I became aware of his almost unnatural presence I could watch how others interacted with him. And most often, apart from an *Alright Dermot* at the start of the evening when he would appear at the fringes of the group, they didn't.

We fell asleep on the sofa that particular evening, the dregs of our wine bottle adding to the reddy-purple colour swirl. Dermot had left at some point during the evening, but neither Emma nor I noticed him go. One moment he was there, then he wasn't.

*

Emma did her best to court him, and—rather infuriatingly as it was *me* I wished she'd turn her attention to—she let me in on every detail. He wasn't shy, she said, he was a step removed from that. And he wasn't melancholy, as some had said—either genuinely or like the faux-goths that hung around outside the library in their designer-vampish clothes—although he didn't laugh at her jokes. Rather, and this was the best way that she could phrase it, he was symbiotic. Not in a parasitical sense, but in a way which led to connections. When she was with him, she felt whole. Just as a party only seemed to come alive when he was present. He added nothing, except completion.

*

I never asked her if they slept together. Eventually, after some persuasion, Emma turned her attentions to me. We did the usual things. Made each other laugh, had sex, eventually moved in with each other and got married. But even after having children there was still something that was missing. I loved Emma and she loved me. However this wasn't enough. We hardly saw Dermot at all, but when we did I always felt myself reaching for Emma's hand.

*

I never planned for it to happen. I was travelling across to Peterborough and she was on the same train. I hadn't taken the car because it had almost failed the MOT and the garage wanted to keep it in overnight. I hate those courtesy cars they fob off on you; it takes me a while to get used to them and when you return to your

181

own car it never quite feels the same. In a way, it was similar to how it might feel if I were to sleep with Emma immediately after having an affair. The difference would be in my head, even if outwardly nothing had changed.

Perhaps this seems a crude analogy, but in this case it's pertinent because on that train journey I met Melanie again.

Some fifteen years had passed since I'd kicked her in the face, but I recognised her immediately. Although she'd obviously filled out in all the right places, it seemed that those additions had simply been hung onto her existing frame. She certainly didn't look as old as me, and whilst her nose appeared a little crooked from where I'd broken it, this only added something to her face. She seemed sexier because of it.

There was one of those immobile tables between us, and my seat faced the direction we were travelling. The other two seats were occupied by the time Melanie boarded, and in fact the train shuddered and began to move as she scanned and re-scanned her ticket. It took her a while, but eventually she asked me if I could swap seats with her.

"I can't travel backwards," she said with a smile.

I returned her smile and we changed seats. Maybe she did recognise me then, I don't know. But what I do know is from that point onwards she was always travelling forwards and I was always going backwards.

*

We fell to talking on the journey. Technically, I'd some work to do on the train for the business meeting I was attending, but I knew

182

the presentation inside out as I'd done it several times before. Melanie pulled a fat Harry Potter out of her bag, but like an anorexic with a salad she never really seemed to touch it. Just dipped into it occasionally, turned her face to the window, and turned her face to me.

We slipped into an easy conversation, although I was careful not to say that I remembered her. She was incredibly attractive, possessing a hint of dark sexuality, with her face framed by long black hair that curled in towards her neck where an Adam's apple would be on a man. I tried to remember if I'd fancied her at school, but the details were hazy. All that came to mind were groups of girls giggling in packs, none of them distinguishable. My main memory was when she was down on the floor. Her eyes frightened, yet also brimming with acceptance. I asked her whether she lived in Peterborough, Norwich, or somewhere in between.

"I've always lived in Norwich," she said, as if it was a surprise that we had never bumped into each other. By the end of the train journey we'd established that I was married and she was single. I don't know whether it was because I'd told a few lies about the marriage, or whether she appreciated those moments which were obviously the truth, but when we left the train we took each other's hands and crossed the road into the Great Northern Hotel opposite the station. It was an antiseptic building, but so, in a way, was the sex.

I ignored the welts that rippled across Melanie's back as I fucked her, the cigarette burns on her upper arms, and the track marks that I thought I could discern in the half-light from the bedside lamp. She wanted me to slap her, and I drew my hand back for what seemed like forever before bringing it down upon her

183

arse. After that first time, it was easy.

*

I had to get a taxi to the meeting, even though it was only fifteen minutes walk up Bright Street. Even then I was almost late, and I thanked God that I knew the presentation inside out. My mouth was on autopilot, my penis was sore from the sex and the position it lay in after I had stuffed it back into my pants, but I was buzzing. Buzzing like I'd never buzzed before.

*

On the train back to Norwich I saw Dermot. He was in the seat in front of me. I could only see the back of his head, but even so, I recognised him. When he raised a hand to scratch at the hairs there, I realised he was wearing a wedding ring. For some reason I found myself smiling. It certainly seemed a day for coincidences. I left my seat so that I could go to the toilet, but really so that I could check on him when I returned.

Whilst I was in the tiny cubicle the train pulled into Ely Station. There is always a sense of disorientation when the train leaves Ely, as it returns some way back along the track it has come before veering off in a new direction. When I'd seen Melanie that morning, we'd actually had to swap seats again at Ely so that she continued to face the direction we were travelling. By that time we were already well acquainted, and she'd pushed her body past mine to get to her seat. That, in a way, had sealed the undercurrent of conversation which had passed between us.

184

But in the toilet the sensation of leaving and returning within moments made me feel faint. Instead of standing to pee, I sat down on the seat. Beads of sweat prickled my forehead, and for a moment I held my face in my hands. I thought of Emma, and how she must never know what I'd done. Pulling Melanie's phone number out of my pocket, I tore the pieces of paper into strips, and then flushed them down the toilet. Even so, I couldn't get rid of the feeling of completeness I had felt when I was with her. I shook my head, and returned to the carriage.

As I passed Dermot's seat, I saw it was now empty. Not only that, but someone was sitting where I had been. Presumably Dermot had left at Ely, and someone else had boarded to take my seat. I glanced up at my briefcase in the overhead rack and seeing that it was still there I decided to take Dermot's seat for the rest of the journey. It was easier than making a fuss. What did it matter where I sat anyway?

The train passed through Thetford and then Attleborough. I found myself losing the sickly feeling and regaining the ability to think rationally. Maybe it was because of its transient nature, but I found that my memories of the sex with Melanie were already fading. If I really thought about it, I could almost convince myself that nothing had happened. That was certainly the state of mind in which I would have to greet Emma when I got home. Destroying Melanie's number made it all the less tangible. Perhaps we genuinely hadn't fucked at all.

Remembering my glimpse of Dermot I took a look at the wedding ring on my own hand.

It wasn't there.

I stared at the impression of a ring on my finger, but even

185

as I looked the indentation seemed to close over, as though I'd never worn a ring at all. I shook my head, rubbed my eyes; all the usual things that one is supposed to do to restore reality. But when I looked again there was no change. Panic rose up in my throat. This was hardly something I could hide from Emma. I tried to remember if I'd taken the ring off when checking into the hotel. Maybe I'd done so subconsciously, diverting any feelings of guilt. But if so, it certainly wasn't in any of my pockets now.

I remembered Melanie then, pulling at my fingers as she led me to bed, a smile on her face that promised all that I eventually took. Had she somehow slipped off my ring in that moment? I thought of the piece of paper with her phone number on it, torn, sodden, and blown all over the Ely tracks.

*

I decided against telling Emma I'd been robbed. It was too complicated, didn't make any sense. I'd only trip myself up over the details. Instead I'd say I removed the ring when washing in the conference centre, that I was trying to remove the traces of thick black marker pen that had stained my hands during the presentation. This wasn't entirely untrue, and as I thought through the idea faint marks appeared on my hands accordingly. The story sounded stupid enough to be believable. I'd pretend to make some calls to the centre to see if anyone had handed in a missing ring. I'd blame a rush to the train, anything, for leaving it on the edge of the sink. I toyed with the idea of saying it fell into the plughole, but dismissed it. She'd want to know why I hadn't called a plumber or someone to retrieve it. Besides, intimating knowledge of its whereabouts felt

186

wrong.

As the train pulled into Norwich I got up ready to leave. I felt redeemed. There was always a crush as the train pulled into the station at this time of day. People just wanted to get home.

Ahead of me, close to the door, I saw the top of Dermot's head through the crowd.

As we left the train I struggled to keep up with him. He kept flipping out of sight, like a smaller fish swimming with larger fish. Weaving in and out, disappearing and reappearing, blinking on and off. Just as I remembered him.

In the car park I saw him enter a Volvo similar to mine. Then I realised my car was still at the garage, so I headed for the taxi rank. In my haste I was first in the queue, and I pretended to the driver that I didn't know the address although I knew the way there. Without him realising, we started to follow Dermot.

*

My mobile beeped a new message as we turned down Riverside Road, but I didn't want any distractions so I ignored it. To my left the river ran alongside us in the opposite direction. I was reminded of Ely Station, and the view of the cathedral over the river on our approach which was then reversed on our return. I remembered sitting on a sofa at a party, then standing in a corner. I remembered a kick in the face, and then a kick in the balls. When Dermot's car turned right at the roundabout and headed up Kett's Hill towards Plumstead Road, I knew he was going to my house and I knew all that I had lost and all that I had gained.

My phone beeped again. A reminder.

Dermot pulled into my drive and the taxi kept going. I thought I could see Emma's reflection behind the glass in the kitchen, but then she became no more than a memory. I didn't tell him to stop, but after a while the taxi pulled over, the driver leaning over the front seats to talk to me.

"Listen mate, I don't mind following other cars around but as we've left him behind, do you mind telling me where we're going?"

I flipped open my mobile and read Melanie's message. *One moment you're in the right group, then you're in the wrong group.*

I'd have to text her to ask her where we lived.

Jump

I stood staring at Serena's front door for several minutes. Previously I'd never noticed the deterioration in the paintwork, but now I saw red flakes littering her step like the shavings from gaudy goldfish. I wondered whether it would be possible to pick them up and replace them like a surrealist jigsaw puzzle. Or whether time and the elements would have curled the slivers and weathered the residue so that they no longer matched. A bit, I thought ruefully, like the relationship between Serena and myself.

A window opened above me and Serena poked her lovely head out of the house.

"Will you piss off," she said. "I've told you that it's over. What more do you want?"

What more did I want? I wanted her to jump with me. That's what I wanted.

*

The downslide all started one evening as we were watching the ITV local news. Presenter Katie Derham had moved over from her usual lunchtime slot and as a result I wasn't paying much attention to what was being said. Katie's hair looked gorgeous that evening, but when a big piece of rock appeared on the backdrop over her left ear Serena dug me in the ribs and I spilt some of my shandy on my trousers. As I wondered whether the stain would come out Serena suddenly stood up and the remains of our takeaway curry fell face first onto the carpet. I was glad we hadn't decided to eat at my flat for once.

"Jesus," Serena said.

But it wasn't the face of Jesus that was on the rock—or meteor as I then realised it was from tuning in to Katie's dulcet voice—it was the destination of humanity itself.

. . . *within six months, and in all probability on the 27ᵗʰ November this year, scientists predict the meteor now christened Doomsday will hit the earth with such incredible force that more than a billion megatons of energy would be released, effectively wiping out all known forms of life. It appears we might finally discover if our assumptions about the extinction of the dinosaurs were correct, even if unfortunately there will be no one alive to document it . . .*

"She's kidding right?"

"It's Katie Derham," I said, "she doesn't kid."

Serena gave me a sudden sideways glance. "Don't think I don't know that you fancy her, Gavin. Jesus! It's the end of the world for chrissakes, it'd be nice if you were thinking of me for a change!"

"Come on," I said. "That's not fair. I ignored your obsession with Mick Hucknall for months."

She flicked the TV off with a fast thumb control that always impressed me.

"Out," she said.

"What?"

"You heard. Out."

"You want me to go?"

"Do I have to spell it O U T *out* to you Gavin?"

"But it's Friday night. The start of the weekend."

She sighed. Her body seemed to ripple as though all her molecules were doing a rather melancholy Mexican wave. "Not many weekends left now, by the sounds of it," she said. "Please go Gavin. I think I want to be alone."

I left that evening knowing that she only *thought* she wanted to be alone. The optimist inside me retained some hope.

*

By the following morning you couldn't get away from it. The meteor was everywhere. On televisions, newspapers, and on placards strapped to the front of the suddenly religious offering us some hope in the afterlife but not a whisper of it beforehand. If I was the *geek* that Serena had often branded me then you'd think I'd be excited by the news, but her temporary rejection had focussed my mind on other matters besides the destruction of everything I knew. If the present was to be even more poignant then I wanted to make the most of the time that I had left. You could do a lot in six months. If only I had the money.

The letterbox rattled as I ate a sandwich that I couldn't remember making. I went to the door and retrieved the local free paper which was remarkably bereft of advertisements. Journalists must be having the time of their lives. I was glad someone was happy. I scanned the pages quickly for anything that might have been new, then turned my attention to the television guide. As expected, all the programmes were meteor-related, either directly or obliquely. Channel Four was showing a series of their Best 100 programmes (movies/songs/sitcoms/one-hit wonders/episodes of EuroTrash/you-name-it-lets-produce-a-list-of-it) as though a countdown for the last generation. Recap what your life was all about so you can live in the past without having to think of the future kind of stuff. It was tempting.

I gave Serena a call.

"It's not over then?" I said, after getting three assurances that our relationship hadn't died.

"I've just told you Gavin. I need some quiet time. This end of the world situation is getting me down. I've only six months left and I want to seriously consider who I want to spend my remaining time with. At the moment that's still you."

I took that as some encouragement.

There was a pause.

"Would you do something for me though?" Another pause. "To prove that you love me?"

"Anything," I said. Knowing that I'd instantly regret it.

"I want you to get rid of your *Devo* records and CDs."

That old chestnut.

Now it was my turn to pause.

"You know what I'm saying don't you Gavin? I want a real man to keep me warm during the last days of my existence, and the word *nerd* comes too easily to my mind when thinking of you. That cheesy 70s band personifies you for me. I'd like to make me . . . I mean you . . . a new man."

192

"But *Devo* were one of the biggest influences on innovative music to emerge from that period," I said, feeling my arguing wheels engage with the familiar tracks and push headlong towards an unstoppable conclusion. "If it wasn't for Devo you wouldn't have had the Pet Shop Boys, the Flaming Lips, or the Aquabats. They were video pioneers. I'd lay money that Kylie's video for 'Can't Get You Out Of My Head' was hugely influenced by Devo . . . "

"Gavin. All that proves is that geeks were influenced by geeks. If you really love me you'd get rid of that stuff and buy me a Simply Red album occasionally. Something to smooch too, not assemble like a plastic toy found in a Kinder egg."

The third time I said *But* she cut me off.

*

I went to work the following Monday as did most of the population. Six months was turning out to be a long wait for the end of the world. You couldn't just sit at home with the curtains drawn. No one had enough food in their freezer to last that long, and if they wanted to get in more stock then there was nothing for it than to work and earn money just as they always did.

Mortgages were defaulted on, however, and after a while the banks didn't seem to mind which was very nice of them. I wished I'd stopped renting when I had the chance but it was too late for that now. Taking a leaf from Channel Four I made up a list of things to do before I died.

1. Make up with Serena;
2. (if that fails stalk Katie Derham).

193

My quieter moments found me analysing just why Serena thought me a geek and whether it mattered. What was so flattering about ungeek qualities anyway? What was so fascinating about gym culture? I didn't even wear glasses for god's sake.

"Have you got rid of those CDs yet?"

I'd followed Serena into *Tesco* and was eyeing the contents of her shopping trolley to check she wasn't buying for two.

"Not yet. Listen, are you serious? You really won't move in with me until I do?"

She brushed some hair out of her eyes. "It's not just that," she said. "But it's a start."

"But we have so little time. I was watching the news today and the most recent attempt to divert the meteor has failed. They were going to fly Bruce Willis out there to dig a hole through it but he's working on a remake of *Moonlighting* and can't get out of his contract."

"Very funny Gavin."

"Come on Serena. I'm the one who's supposed to be serious, remember. Don't be downhearted."

She shook her head in disbelief. "We're all going to die Gavin."

"We were always going to die."

"Tell that to them," she said, and pointed to the queue of people standing behind us. Some of them looked angry. One of them spoke up.

"Leave her alone, baldy. It's people like you that got us into this mess in the first place."

Baldy! That was a new one. I took a quick account of the guy's physique and decided I'd rather pick on someone my own

194

size.

"I'll call you," I said; knocking over a display of tinned peas as I forced my way through to the exit.

*

Five months on desperation had set in. I'd relinquished my Devo collection to Oxfam after none of the second-hand record stores would take it, but Serena still refused to move in with me for the last month of our existence. There was always something else, another piece of me to discard before she'd take me on, another concession to make. I began to wonder if there was *someone* else. Whether this meteor business was just an excuse to end what I had thought was something special.

Not that I'd ploughed a fallow field in the intervening period. There was that one date with the Katie Derham lookalike I found on the www.sleepwithsomeonebeforeyoudie.com website, although when I'd turned up and said *Nice to meteor* I realised that I'd made a bad first impression.

"Ay?"

I remembered Serena once saying that just because someone doesn't laugh doesn't mean they didn't get the joke, so I deferred from a lengthy explanation and spent the rest of the evening wondering if understanding me might have tipped the balance. As it was, the only thing that came out of the date was the realisation that we might stop the end of the world after all?

"Have you signed up to jump?"

It was my turn to put on a puzzled-face. Almost a monkey puzzled face. I wondered whether there was some kind of queuing system for nookie on the dating website that I'd skipped over in my rush for a shallow experience.

"Er . . . "

She looked me hard in the eyes, and just for the moment she *was* Katie Derham. "You've got to do it you know. It's our only chance."

"Our only chance . . . ?"

"Don't you see? Mankind finally has the option to choose life over death, but it has to be a unanimous decision. Well, a tenth of the population anyhow but that's not much different from the average election turnouts is it? Everyone who doesn't register has the blood of humanity on their hands."

I hadn't a clue what she was talking about. At that precise moment there was something else I wanted to have on my hands. Even if her Katie resemblance only began and ended at her face. I'd take that chance.

"Jump where," I said, lamely.

"Where do you think," she said scornfully. "Downwards?"

We went our separate ways shortly after that and although I was tempted to lodge a formal complaint with the agency that my date had been nothing more than a propagandist canvassing at the lowest possible level of opportunity, I didn't. It would say too much about me and not enough about her.

Yet I'd kept the card and leaflet she'd given me, and it wasn't long—as soon as I got back home, soaked to the skin from a sudden downpour—that I'd logged on to the appropriate website and read the information provided. After several hours I still couldn't be sure if it was a joke. There were so many meteor-prevention theories out there that few could be trusted to have any basis in scientific reality, but there was something about this one that made it alluring. Maybe I could win Serena back through one instant of physical exercise rather than a final month in the gym?

In theory the idea was simple. The organisers of *Jump Against Doomsday* required 600 million people to jump simultaneously exactly one week before the rock was due to hit. Scientific research had *proven* that planet earth could be driven out of its current orbital rotation by the combined force of human beings jumping in the Western Hemisphere at a given time, thus shifting the earth away from the meteor's path—admittedly by a hair's breadth. Not only that, but the new orbit was likely to be of benefit against global warming too.

So far, 578,970,189 people had put their names down for the task. I was the five hundred and seventy eight millionth nine hundred and seventy thousandth one hundred and ninetieth person to take part. For some reason the possibility that being a number might lead to being a free man excited me. I wrote my number down and kept it in my wallet should anyone ask me what it was.

Then I phoned Serena.

*

"You *are* joking?"

"No. I'm not joking. I'm surprised it hasn't been on the news."

"And you've really signed up for this?"

"It's our future I'm thinking about Serena."

I thought I could detect a snort at the end of the line, but I was feeling good about myself and decided to file it as a cough.

"Gavin. I've told you what I want from you. I want someone to sweep me off my feet, not jump me off my feet. Someone with a bit of balls."

"If it's musculature you're after," I found myself saying, "then why don't you hang out at the *Meat Market* or one of the other Friday night clubs for the over 30s? You'd find you'd be getting your pantry full there, but are you sure it isn't me that you want to bring home the bacon?"

That was definitely a snort.

"I'm sorry Gavin, but I've become resigned to the fact that the world is ending and it might well be a better place if everyone else did the same thing. These cockahoopie theories and escape routes aren't for me. And neither, now you've reminded me of your sense of humour, are you."

"It's cockamamie," I said.

"What?"

"It's cockamamie theories, not cockahoopie."

When she hung up it sounded as though there were a hundred party-line listeners laughing at me from the void.

*

So there we have it. The end of the world in precisely one week and two hours time, and my final attempt to make Serena see sense ended a few minutes ago with her door in my face. That red paint will do more than flake when the meteor hits anyway. The minutiae of life won't matter anymore. The pulp of the world against the canvas of the universe will be the bigger painted picture.

I'd contacted Serena at least a dozen times since she'd first refuted the idea of jumping, all with no success. To be honest, I'd given up on the whole idea, until I logged onto the Jump Against Doomsday website this morning just before heading to my assigned jump spot. The number of registered participants had halted at 599,999,999. Serena might have made the difference. But there was no chance of that now.

*

I looked up at her window one last time. The corolla of her blond frizzy hair was silhouetted against an incredible glare of light in the sky above her. That didn't look right to me. Regardless of where she might be getting her hair products from. Almost simultaneously a series of shouts erupted along the row of terraces as televisions leaked the news the world's governments had been holding back. The meteor was due to hit today, one week earlier than predicted. The information had been previously withheld to prevent last minute looting. Or at least, that was the reason behind it that Serena told me as she relayed the broadcast from her bedside portable to me on the street below.

There was a pause.

"I'm coming down," she said.

We took off towards the park, our hearts pounding. I wished we were there under different circumstances but there was still a chance that we might be in the future if that crazy plan just worked.

The central grassy area was packed. There was no one on the swings, but an endless sea of people stretched out to the horizon. Serena gave me a kiss and I noticed that she was wearing the

199

fragrance that I'd bought for her the previous Christmas. The one that she always told me she never liked.

Then there was another pause. One that ran worldwide.

We synchronised our watches.

Holding Serena's hand in mine, we jumped.

I just hoped that the meteor wouldn't hit whilst we were hanging in the air.

The Strangeness in Me

When you've got the blues, who do you tell them to?
When you're all alone, what do you want to do?
Do you want to die, or is it the strangeness in me?

The image of his dead wife had been with him for such a long time that if Montgomery closed his eyes he might convince himself that he had killed her. Then he would step out of the reverie and realise she was still alive.

Whilst he knew there was no such thing, it felt as if he was trapped inside a breathing heart. With each inhalation the walls of the heart stretched, became transparent. In those moments he could almost see out, could see the sides of the heart touching something. Then the breath left him again.

He looked out of the window. The train bumped its way across the landscape. Cornfields brushed against the sides of the engine. In the distance, he could see children playing. The sun bore down like a wax seal, imprinting itself on everything.

Montgomery pulled a handkerchief out of his pocket and

wiped his forehead. It was easy to imagine that the train was stationary. That the scenery rolled by as if painted on canvas, turned by burly men in the wings. Was it the grime on the glass, or where there flecks on the horizon indicative of brushstrokes? Montgomery's grasp on reality seemed to be slipping with greater regularity as he got older. He knew that it was a subterfuge, a method that worked to convince himself that one day he wouldn't die.

Or maybe it was dying alone that he was afraid of. Although sometimes he felt that there was two of him.

He splayed out his hands on the table. His skin held the waxy sheen of a plucked chicken, puckered with the wrinkles of age. When he moved his fingers they resembled bodies under thin sheets.

It wasn't like this in the movies. Film stars had their own brand of immortality, fixed in time and space. Yet by encapsulating himself within the pretence of an alternate reality wasn't he attempting to attain the same status? If everything was indeed a conceit then there had to be a plot, a plan to it all. Whilst he acknowledged this might be no more than the security blanket of most religions, the artifice of it intrigued him. Actors know they are acting, but simultaneously their characters are unaware of the film's constraints. Watching them after their deaths kept them alive in the imagination. And wasn't that all we were after all? Alive in other people's imaginations?

Even at eighty there was so much that he didn't know.

On the other side of the compartment a couple were seated across a low table. The man put down the book that he had been reading and nudged the woman's elbow. She looked up, looked away from the window. Montgomery knew they were about to start a conversation and he reached into his jacket pocket for some paper and his pen. He kept slips of paper, three inches square, on his person at all times. The couple's voices were low, almost indistinct, then he heard:

I'm asking you to marry me, you little fool.

He wrote the words down on the paper.

I'm not the sort of woman men marry.

The couple glanced over to Montgomery, tried to keep the conversation down. Their eyes, their expressions, told the remainder of the story, but Montgomery couldn't get to grips with those kinds of signs. He re-read the words on the paper, then slipped them into the plastic carrier bag at his feet. It was stuffed, almost overflowing, with similar sized pieces of paper.

Montgomery sighed. What intimidated him more than imagining his wife dead, was wondering whether he actually wanted her to cease existing. Being dead in his head was no doubt quite different from being dead in reality. *Removed*, might better express his desire. And removing something meant placing it somewhere else, didn't it; rather than eradicating it completely. It was true that a dead body finds its place in the ground, or in the air as ash and smoke, but Montgomery believed that character went nowhere. Even centuries of arguments about the soul differed over the role of the mind.

He held his head in his hands. Why couldn't life be like that Hitchcock movie, *Strangers on a Train*, when one of the passengers took on the crimes of another, creating a perfect alibi? Trains were the favourite places for his reveries, the rhythm of the journey conjuring semi-sleep states of consciousness, of imagination. Fantasy born from monotony, unlike his marriage which had been the other way round.

Eve had been a different kind of woman. But then she became every woman.

She was thirty years his junior when he met her, almost ten years ago. Brash, blonde, sultry; tawdry at times. Montgomery knew that his money attracted her, but physically they had coupled all the same. Maybe he had convinced himself, but he always believed that there was *something* there, a spark between them. It wasn't as if she was a very good actress. He had seen those early movies.

Given hindsight he now wished that he hadn't. But he had. He had asked her to marry him too. Begged it with a passion that embarrassed him whenever he thought about it. The fact that she kept turning him down only made him persist. No doubt that was what she was after, to make it appear that she wasn't too easy. She even took the moral highground . . .

What's wrong with me?

You don't believe in marriage.

I've been married twice.

See what I mean.

Montgomery bent his head to look down the aisle of the train. A rotund man was in conversation with a younger, slightly shorter male. Both of them were balding, although the younger man had his hair cut short as if to disguise the fact. As Montgomery watched them their conversation stalled, they turned towards him. He kept his gaze forwards, knowing that to look away might arouse suspicion. After a few seconds the men shook hands and returned to their seats. Montgomery hadn't been able to catch any of the conversation.

On many a journey Montgomery had regarded his fellow

passengers, desirous that they might approach and offer to kill his wife. They came in all shapes and sizes, but there was always one with a weasel face and thin moustache. A potential killer if ever there was one. Surely they would be up for it? Montgomery had trampled over a lot of people to get where he was today—in the position that a younger, more attractive wife could also walk all over him. So it couldn't be that difficult, could it? Not that weasel-face seemed to be on this train. The absence of mirrors acquitted his memory.

The adjacent couple had stopped their conversation, with the man returning to his book. The cover was folded around the back, and from where he sat Montgomery couldn't see the title. This began to bother him. Perhaps it might have some relevance. He was often dogged by coincidence, again adding to the presumption that all wasn't quite as random as it should be. As though there was a script to be followed. Scenes to be kept to.

The woman was looking out of the window. She was smartly dressed in a pink suit, her legs were bare. Montgomery guessed she was in her late thirties, perhaps later. He could draw comparisons with Eve, his wife, but he derailed his thinking from that track. Instead he focussed on the unknown woman, realised how easy it would be to kill her.

When he imagined his wife dead, regardless of whether he believed he had killed her, the act had already taken place. Uxoricide—he had looked it up on the Internet—didn't sit right with him, imagined or otherwise. Perhaps this was borne from an inherent morality that insisted that he wouldn't have been able to perform the task himself. But there was no such complication when it came to bumping off another person's wife.

It wasn't only morality or the fear that he might be caught that stopped him from despatching Eve. They had an attachment —of sorts—after all. But to kill a person that he hadn't met prior to that moment . . . within his insular reality it wouldn't matter, would it? They would go from not being there—in his circle of association —to simply *not being there.* Thousands of people died daily. What did they matter to him? It was only the personal connection which rooted his wife in his consciousness after all. But a stranger. That was different. If he was completely unaware of a stranger before killing them, then he couldn't miss them when they died. It stood to reason.

Yet, despite all of the incentives, Montgomery knew that it was something else to approach anyone and ask. He'd have to sit and wait, whilst the countryside rushed passed him through the glass, and hawks screamed in the air above them. And if he had to wait for a complete stranger to tap him on the shoulder and suggest topping his wife, then he had the feeling he'd have a very long wait indeed.

*

When your heart is sad, do you not want to die?
When your baby's gone, do you get up with a sigh?
Do you want to weep, or is it the strangeness in me?

*

They were approaching the Eastern Seaboard. Elizabeth City in North Carolina, to be precise. And from there Montgomery had decided to make his way to Kill Devil Hills, so-named from a brand of rum that had got washed ashore there during colonial times. It seemed fitting, somehow. Montgomery had lost many of his days to drink.

Are you not happy with your life?

Montgomery looked up. The stewardess faced him, leaning across the top of a trolley bearing a selection of pastries, carbonated drinks, and potato chips. Her hair was tucked into a short, white cap. She was smiling like she didn't mean to. As if she was on camera.

I'm sorry?

I said, 'are you not happy with your life'? Is there someone you would like me to kill?

Montgomery shook his head. His mouth was dry. He wanted to ask for some bottled water, but he felt twelve years old and awkward. She wasn't beautiful, far from it, but she intimidated him with her looks. There was something tangible about her, something compelling, other than her physical being.

She was still looking at him.

If I let you change me, will that do it? If I do what you tell me, will you love me?

Montgomery had a pain in his chest. He couldn't breath. Desperately he tried to speak, to say something, but the words wouldn't come. He became aware of his hands, pressed against the tabletop. The grain of the wood emulated his fingerprints. Someone inside him laughed, but the waitress didn't hear it. She took his silence literally, and pushed her trolley down the aisle without looking back.

The temporary paralysis left him and he reached into his

plastic carrier, pulling out a handful of paper. As his fingers regained some feeling he turned the fragments round and around. His heart was steady. He must have imagined that he hadn't been breathing. Taking out his handkerchief he mopped his brow again. Before replacing it in his pocket he looked at the thin white hairs that clung to the fabric. He felt sick.

He wondered whether any of Eve's hairs were attached to him. Woven into the material of his jacket, burrowing into the cloth. He had always been aware that when we touch someone a part of them comes away with us.

Montgomery flicked the pieces of paper around on the tabletop. Scraps of conversation. They were art. Never mind the discussions over paintings, sculpture, performance pieces, any of the modern form. *Is it art?* wasn't a question that concerned him. A dead body was art. Anything was art when it was removed from its original context. For Montgomery, viewing life from an alternate perspective was art. And this was symbiotic: you couldn't separate the viewer from the art. Art had to be viewed to determine its existence as such. In viewing art, you created yourself.

One of the pieces of paper fell from the table into his lap. He picked it up, read it:

She wants me to marry her.
That's normal.
I don't want to.
That's abnormal.

Montgomery couldn't recall the people the conversation related to, or when he had written it down. But the source no longer mattered. It was part of him now. It assisted in making him, just as all the other pieces of paper made him.

Eve was something different. Eve had unmade him. As though his soul consisted of a single piece of cotton she had seen a thread and unpicked him. He didn't doubt that she had affairs, despite the lack of proof. For the thirty year age gap it was almost a necessity. It would be like having ribs without barbecue sauce, or a splash of water without a shot of Jack Daniels. Quite simply, it was one of those things.

Montgomery had no intentions of going to jail, and no inclination to tell anyone his feelings. Those flunkies he surrounded himself with were no better than the rest. The children from his first marriage were worse. In order to reciprocate, to unmake his wife, he had to unmake himself.

*

I thought I'd said goodbye, I won't be seeing you no more
Already I have tried, I spent long hours on the floor
Should I try to leave, or bring back the strangeness in me?

*

Montgomery left the train at Elizabeth City and looked for a bus to the Outer Banks. On Hughes Boulevard he bought a ticket to Kill Devil Hills on a Greyhound that was leaving in an hour. The weather was cooling down, the late summer evening dissipating the heat. He was getting hungry, but instead he headed down to the waterfront and looked out over the Pasquotank River, at the spot where it opened up and began widening out on its course to the Albemarle Sound.

He watched a procession of young girls make their way along the wooden walkways that threaded through Memorial Park. Their skirts flicked at the tops of their thighs. The weight of the paper in his carrier bag was nothing compared to the weight of the words.

As if men don't desire strangers!

Montgomery jerked his head around but Eve was nowhere to be seen. He ran a hand through his hair. Then slid it onto his face, rubbed his eyes. If he looked through his fingers, if he peeked, might he not see the spool of the film reel running up the sides of his vision?

What was it with that movie? *Strangers on a Train*? One of the characters had suggested the murders, and the other had thought it a joke, yet wasn't it a fact that once something is imaginable it becomes possible? After all, in a sense, wasn't that how science worked? Nothing is discovered, simply created. We are the gods of own imaginations.

So was that how it happened? Montgomery remembered her body lying on the floor of their penthouse apartment. It was ironic that she was on the ground even though they were thirty stories up in the air. In the corner of the room he could see the telephone cord, extended way beyond its flexibility. More irony: she had always been the one against a cordless phone. Always wanting to entwine the cord around her finger as she spoke. Just as she had wound and then unwound him.

Wound. With dialogue, in a movie, pronunciation could be everything.

Her face was in close-up. Eyes wild. Her blond hair con-trasted with the red-lipsticked bruise that had purple pulsing be-

210

neath it. Her legs were crossed at the knee.

A memory or a reverie? If it was imagined, then had it been created? He felt sick again. It was knowledge. Knowledge made him ill. Whenever he needed something done it was always done in shadow. *Don't tell me about it, just do it.* The number of things he hadn't been told about for him to get where he was today.

But this was different. He told himself this.

When the sun went down and before the lights went up, everything was black and white.

Montgomery boarded the Greyhound for the short journey to Kill Devil Hills. There was something prophetic in the name, although he hadn't chosen it at random. The site was the place where the Wright brothers had taken their first heavier-than-air flight in 1903. Imagination had created the ability to fly. There wasn't any other way to view it.

The bus was full. Montgomery found himself pressed against a young man, possibly Hispanic, who constantly leant forwards to speak to a girl sitting diagonally opposite. Their conversation was worth recording, but he couldn't write it down because there was nothing to lean against in the cramped space. Instead he flicked through the remnants of dialogue in his carrier bag. Made up an alternate conversation from snippets of time passed:

Poor unfortunate girl.

She was a tramp.

She was a human being. Let me remind you that even the most unworthy of us has a right to life and the pursuit of happiness.

Not many people left the bus at Kill Devil Hills. Montgomery waited for those that did to disperse, and then he began to walk towards the beach. He was being shadowed, he knew that. His character, a subsequent part of himself that had been created by Eve, dogged his every step. He had asked himself to commit a murder, and he had done so. Now it was time for the exchange.

Montgomery saw the scene as if from above, marvelling at its cinematic beauty. The beach was deserted, dark. Waves could be heard on the soundtrack, alternately crashing then receding. He sat on the grass-covered dunes, and then pushed himself off. Standing to his feet he began to walk across to the sea, the pressed sand undulating under the soles of his Brogues.

At the water's edge he slipped his shoes off, wondered whether whoever found them would bother to remove the tiny stones that were embedded in the grooves. And if so, what they would do with them afterwards.

He recalled standing beside his father on Coney Island. It must have been a very long time ago. His father, tall and gaunt, lent down stiffly and picked up a stone. It was as though the effort might break him in half. Turning the stone over in his hands he had rubbed the surface, as if making it smooth, before arcing his arm back and then sharply forwards. With a final twist of the wrist he sent it skimming across the waves.

Montgomery remembered thinking what a desolate thing it was to do. And he'd told him so.

Behind them, the fun fair had twinkled; turned.

In the here and now Montgomery looked down at his feet. The thought of sand pressing into the spaces between his toes made him squirm. He decided to keep his socks on. He didn't want to return sand to the ocean, to displace the scene. Instead he removed his jacket, then unbuttoned his shirt, laid them out neatly on the ground. Slipping out of his trousers he became aware of the fragility of his body. Removing his underpants was a revelation.

He picked up the carrier bag. So many memories. Where they his private property or did they belong to the populace? Just like *Hansel and Gretel* he had retained them to follow himself back home, to thread through the circuitous meandering of his consciousness to the point at which he imagined he had come into being. But if Eve were not dead he would be kept alive within her imagination. And if she was dead, then he needed to follow her. It was quite simply the way things were written.

Grasping the bottom of the bag Montgomery lifted it high into the air and shook it. Gravity and the wind emptied the contents over the sea, scattering like tickertape confetti. Montgomery walked into that same sea, littered with his imaginings. At the last moment, when the waves bobbed his body to the extent that he could barely keep his feet on the ground, he slipped off his socks and folded one inside the other. Then threw them back to join the remainder of his clothes on the beach. Where they belonged.

He would be okay. He only had himself to blame.

Love is the Drug

What has to happen for perfection to no longer be enough?

Start at the beginning, John.

"The beginning? Whenabouts? You want me to go right back to my childhood?"

Not your childhood, John. Everyone is mixed up in their childhood, assimilating information, assembling themselves. Start at puberty: that's where it all begins to make sense.

So I started at puberty for him, but I didn't start at puberty for me. Because I knew precisely when it began to go wrong. The answers were already inside me. Circulating within my bloodstream.

*

I was just a regular guy. Typically married, three kids, no worries. Life was just peachy. As it was for everyone. Living the Earth dream. I caught the 'Scape to work every morning at 9am sharp, performed my job in the city to perfection, and returned home using the 'Turn bang on 6pm. Dinner was more often than not on

214

the table. The kids were scrubbed and clean, and if not ready for bed then gradually getting there. My wife greeted me with a kiss and a smile.

Weekends we'd take a drive out to the coast. The skies were a clear blue, imposing yet forever friendly wind-turbines adding a sharpened whiteness to the view that made it all the more crisp and fresh. We'd lie back on sunloungers, suitably protected, and watch through our shades as the kids took to the sea. Squealing and running and splashing.

We'd light up a joint and get all warm and comfortable. Through the smoke haze and the heat haze we'd relax, hands held, our minds spiralling away as we dozed, the sounds of the kids echoing off the sea, laughter and happiness filling our ears. Experiencing the well-being that we were accustomed to. That everyone was accustomed to.

On those weekend evenings, after the kids were in bed, we'd break open a bottle of wine, plug ourselves into the Max, and enjoy a bit of *RealTime* with our friends. Later, making love, Judy would gasp softly, quietly, biting back her cries so that the kids wouldn't wake. It was then that I'd let myself go—her controlled orgasms touching me somewhere base, kicking me into life, firing up the cylinders and jettisoning me into space. At least, that's how it felt as we hugged together afterwards, ripples of happiness coursing through our bodies.

*

John?

"Hmmm?"

I can feel you going off topic John. Our sensors are picking up some extraneous activity.

"What do you want me to do?"

Go back to the incident, John. You know which one I mean.

"But if you know all this . . ."

Just go back.

*

I remembered it clearly enough, there was no point pretending that I didn't. I'd been allocated a time-owed afternoon. Occasional short lunch hours, staying a little later than usual: it had all added up. A memo had popped up on my digital medium. I suddenly had an hour to kill. Not that I had many options. The Turns wouldn't be running until after six, and an hour wasn't enough to do anything exciting. I decided to go for a quick stroll. The sun was out and the streets wouldn't be congested this time of day. Not only that, but we were running out of pot, and it would be an opportunity to source another supply.

I removed my jacket as I left the building, hooked my fingers into the collar and slung it over my shoulder. Loosened my tie too. It was a glorious day. It was always a glorious day. But that never tainted my appreciation. There were only a handful of people walking around the square near our offices. I sat for a while on a bench and closed my eyes, the sun turning my vision gold, a few birds calling to each other in the trees above me. As ever, I was immensely content. Life was good, kind. Everything was always going to be okay.

After a while I wandered across the square and looked for

my usual dope dealer. Despite it being legalised there was still a tradition of buying on street corners. I guessed old habits die hard. But my usual vendor wasn't about. I turned on the spot, puzzled, raked a hand through my hair. Then shrugged. It was no problem. I would have to go without. We still had a little left as it was.

"Looking for something?"

I turned, surprised. A guy stood before me, his palms flat and open in the international sign of friendship. A green cloth bag hung over his shoulder.

"Just my usual supplier. Don't know if you've seen him around? A short guy, beard . . . "

He waved at me dismissively. "I'm new here, don't know anyone. But I have stuff."

He opened the top of the bag and I saw a few coloured packages. None of them looked like dope.

"What are you looking for?"

I shrugged. "I don't know. The usual, I guess."

"I can better that." He reached into the bag and pulled out a small clear parcel, no bigger than a rat's fist. It contained a pale green powder. Not enough for one joint.

"No thanks." I felt uneasy.

"Don't you want to know what it is?"

I found myself looking around. Shrugged again. "Go on."

"It's Conflict."

*

So John, what did you think of that?
    "I could remember it."

217

Context?

"I recalled it from school. I remember being told there were three essential elements to a story: character, scene, and conflict. Character and scene still made sense of course, but I didn't remember much about conflict."

What did he tell you?

"That it would give me feelings I hadn't had before." I started getting agitated, held my head in my hands.

It's okay John. We're here to help you. Continue.

*

There had been so little in the packet that I didn't mention it to Judy when I got home. There wasn't enough for both of us, and I reasoned if it was good then I could buy two packets the following day. Judy deserved a little treat. It was her birthday coming up and I wanted her to feel extra special.

Once she was asleep I slipped out to the toilet and snorted the powder into my nose. The vendor mentioned a slight tingling sensation and he was right. I looked at myself in the mirror, not sure what to expect. After a while I got bored, turned out the light, and made my way back to our room.

I slept fitfully.

Judy was already awake when I woke. I heard her in the kitchen, preparing breakfast for our kids. I yawned and stretched. My eyes were wet. I wiped the sleepy out and thought about getting out of bed. But I stayed there awhile. Thinking.

Something was gnawing within me.

Judy usually woke me. But she hadn't. What was this?

My head was fuzzy. I rubbed my eyes again. I had a feeling in the centre of my stomach that I couldn't describe.

*

Wait John. Try and describe it now.
"Now? Now is easy. Loss and longing."
Go on.

*

I sat up and dressed disconsolately. Did I have a cold? I didn't believe that I did. There was a pain inside my chest, but it wasn't physical. At least, it didn't seem to be. When I stood I was dizzy.

I remembered the drug. Deliberated whether to tell Judy about it. Decided against it. We always shared everything but she didn't need to know. I turned that thought over in my mind. But I was right. She didn't need to know.

I finished getting dressed, mildly annoyed that I couldn't find two socks that matched, and wandered into the breakfast room.

"Morning babe. You were sleeping so soundly I didn't want to wake you." Judy was smiling, pouring milk over cornflakes for the kids.

"You always wake me."

There was an edge to my voice. Terse. Something flickered over Judy's face, an expression that cut me up at the same time as it pleased me.

"Sorry." Her voice fluctuated as she spoke. I realised she'd

219

never said that word to me before. Ever. She'd never had to say it.

I grunted. Pulled over a bowl of cornflakes and started to eat. The milk seemed super sweet, the mush of flakes in my mouth were hard to swallow. I poured out some coffee but it was too bitter. I got up from the table without finishing them. Noticed Judy trying not to watch me.

In the bathroom I looked at myself in the mirror. Nothing seemed different. It was just me looking back. The *me* that always looked back. I suddenly felt empty. I wanted to go back to the breakfast room and hold Judy, feel her warmth, her love. But instead I kept looking into the mirror and wondered what life might be like without her. When I cleaned my teeth I gagged, vomited the cornflakes and milk and coffee into the basin. Then cleaned my teeth again.

I kissed her goodbye as usual but it was just habit.

On the 'Scape into work my eyes wandered from female to female. I felt that I was looking for something, making a composite woman from the bit parts of others. The back of a hand, skin smooth, knuckles like aureole. Calves encased in thin woollen tights. Blue eyes. A stance. The corner of a potential smile.

I felt I was looking for something but I didn't know what it was.

*

I'm going to stop you one more time John. One more time after this time.

"Okay."

This emotion you were feeling. Was it pleasant?

"Pleasant? I'm not sure if I could describe it as pleasant."

But there were elements of pleasure?

"No." I rubbed my eyes hard, encouraging clarity. "Dissatisfaction. That was what I felt. If there was pleasure, it was only a promise at the end of all this."

At the end of all what, John.

"At the end of my marriage."

*

I'd been useless in the office that day. My mind wandered. I was vague when it came to answering queries. I found I wasn't listening to what people were saying. I found that I didn't care what people were saying. And when my boss took me into his office I found that I didn't care what he was saying either.

I stood there looking out of the window. I could see the square. There was a central statue overlooked by lawns and benches. A few people were milling about. They didn't seem to have any purpose other than for me to watch them whilst I was told about call back times, figures, marketing criteria. None of it was relevant.

I clenched and unclenched my fists. I had a sense of urgency coupled with impossibility. But not futility. I knew I had a decision to make that would free me, but I wasn't sure how that decision could be.

And so it went on.

Each day started the same. I'd wake up and there would be a moment of clarity, everything right with the world. Then I'd notice Judy, sleeping with her back to me. Something would crumble. I'd watch my arm reach out to touch her, hold her, then pull back. I longed for the contact, but had a fear of improving the fragile situation that existed between us. It would be a step back from where I was. A step that I couldn't take. So I'd lie there, becoming increasingly frustrated. My forehead would tighten, as though a band had been fitted around it during the night. Sometimes water even came out of my eyes. It seemed wrong but it also seemed right.

The kids, too, were more of an irritant than a pleasure. They were noisy, asked stupid questions, got in my way, under my feet. And through all this I could see myself clearly, stumbling along without direction or conviction, seemingly powerless to do anything about it. Caught up in emotions I hadn't known to exist.

*

I'm going to stop you one more time John. One more time after this time.

"You said that last time."

I need to stop you because you're trying to rationalise. We don't need that. We need facts. We need you to tell us what happened this morning.

"I'm getting to that."

You're going round in circles, trapped in a spiral of self-destruction. You won't find the answers there.

"So what do you want?"

What do you want?

"Release."

Tell us what happened this morning.

*

I'd got on the 'Scape. I'd hoped to find a seat. My palms were sweating. I was dizzy again, my forehead was cold and I thought I'd collapse. I recognised symptoms from previous illnesses, but this was an emotional breakdown. I acknowledged that now, rather than taking each feeling in turn, analysing it. I could only describe it as a breakdown. Like the 'Scape might breakdown occasionally. That was the analogy I had.

I clung to the pole in the carriage, my eyes closed, independent of the people around me. I knew some of the passengers, either as neighbours or in the daily commute, but I spoke to no one and no one spoke to me. I couldn't speak to anyone. Whenever I thought about contact I had a prickling sensation behind my eyes and the band on my head tightened.

Last night Judy had persuaded me to plug into the Max. I could tell what she was trying to do. To reconnect me with everyone, with her. To my great surprise, water came out of her eyes too. When we went to bed we didn't touch, didn't offer even a placatory *goodnight*. The situation had to stop. I knew it.

So when I left the 'Scape I didn't go to work. I stood in the square with my arms outstretched and spun around, trying to catch sight of the vendor. And when I couldn't see him, I began screaming. One, long, open-mouthed exclamation of everything that was pent up inside me. Windows opened, people stopped on their way to work. I was watched. But even in this act of release, I wasn't a free man.

And then you came.

*

Do you know why I'm here?

"To get rid of the Conflict?"

I'm afraid that's not possible John. Only you can do that.

I held my head in my hands.

In any event John, Conflict as a drug doesn't exist.

I looked up. "But that's what he gave me."

He didn't give you 'Conflict', he gave you 'Love'. But you already had Love. That's the conflict.

"Love?"

When you say 'I love you' to your children, to your wife, you're expressing a conditioned and non-emotional response. The love you were given is subversive.

"I want it out of me."

It isn't there. It left your bloodstream days ago. Your body cells have become addicted to creating a vicious circle of reoccurring emotional situations and states. You're perpetuating those states yourself through repetition. That's how emotion works. Real emotion.

I remembered Judy, the kids. Then realised it was only remembering.

I thought of seeing them, tried to visualise them. But that was only a memory too.

Then I thought of what was inside me: the feelings of longing and loss, of hopeful attainment, of reaching out towards something that I didn't even know was there, but wanting it more desperately and permanently than anything I'd ever wanted before.

My eyes were wet again.

I rubbed them. Held my palms out.

"What are these?"

Those are tears, John.

224

He leant forward and I fell into him, my body convulsing,
my mind screwed, tears falling, falling down my face.
That's it John, let it out. Let out the love.
And as I did I knew those feelings would stay.

Chasing Waterfalls

Julia loved the twins.

Platonically.

At least, she did at the beginning. Then, just as the twins' zygote had divided to form separate embryos, so Julia's affections had also split in two. Often she was the only person who could tell them apart. As time went by she found it increasingly harder to hide her feelings. Until the moment that everything changed.

*

Carl and Ralf were at work in their garage in Buffalo. They lived in the white-painted colonial house that previously belonged to their parents. Three stories high, the building rose in stages like an oriental pagoda, with the twins spending most of their time either in the topmost room, which overlooked Colvin Avenue and from which they had a good view of anyone approaching the building, or within the garage. Their pick-up was usually parked out front, as the garage was filled with all manner of equipment that only they seemed to know what to do with.

Julia always found them building stuff. Whether it had anything to do with their twin sensibilities or simple sibling connections she was perpetually fascinated that they never had to instruct each other what to do. One would pick up a screw, the other the screwdriver, as though a simultaneous action. In the same way, whatever they were building was gradually constructed. Without plans or—in many instances—purpose. Often when they finished they just looked at it for a few days before taking it apart again.

When Julia knocked on the side of the garage that morning the sun was shining and the sounds of the twins humming filled the air. At first they were so absorbed in their work that they didn't hear her, and she held back from knocking a second time so that she might observe them.

To describe one would be to describe them both. They were identical twins, the fact that Carl had been born a few moments before Ralf was almost all that separated them. Six foot tall, short blond hair, rugged features, awkwardly handsome, bright blue eyes. They usually wore blue denims and checked shirts and today was no different. Julia saw them bent over some kind of cylindrical object, smoothing the surface down. It could have been a giant bullet, or maybe a cannon. Carl was closer to her. She never knew quite how she could tell, but she could. In many instances, it was always Ralf who seemed to be further away.

She rapped on the side of the garage again. A squirrel that was on the roof leapt up onto the first floor balcony of the house. As its paws touched the polished wooden floor Carl and Ralf looked up at Julia. Both of them smiled.

"Hey, how's it going?"

It was Carl who spoke first, with Ralf's identical remark almost like an echo between them. They often spoke simultaneously, although it was only the standard phrases that tended to be identical.

"I'm fine." Julia smiled. "What is it you're building today?"

Ralf grinned. "We haven't got a name for it yet, but it'll sure be something."

Carl nodded. "It has a purpose too," he said. "We know exactly what we'll be doing with this one."

Julia entered the garage, her eyes adjusting to the darkness in comparison with the bright sunlight outdoors. The object was at least four, maybe five feet long. It could have been a metal barrel, yet there was something about it that meant she knew it wasn't an ordinary container. The twins had been sanding down the sides, making it as smooth as possible. It looked sleek and exciting. Then she saw a similar object standing upright in the corner.

She tilted her head in its direction. "Another one?"

Carl nodded. "That's the second one. This is the first."

"Watcha going to do with them?"

Ralf tapped the side of his nose. "That's for us to know and for you to find out."

Julia walked around the other side of the work bench. The garage walls were festooned with a wide variety of tools and materials, all in very specific places. It was the tidiest, yet busiest, garage she had ever seen.

"It's a lovely day out there. No one wants to go for a drive?"

She knew that Carl would look at her first. Not straight on, but out of the corner of his eye. He hesitated, but then Ralf beat

228

him to it.

"We have work to do."

"So I see. But it's such a nice day."

Carl looked at her directly then, holding her gaze. "Ralf's right, Julia, we have work to do. We've got plans."

Julia jerked her head backwards, made a sniffing sound. She pretended she was upset at being snubbed, but really she had expected no other answer from them. Inside her, deep inside like a mudskipper waiting rain, she knew that eventually her time would come. She'd lure Carl away from Ralf and they'd be happy together. It was just that Carl didn't know it yet, but as soon as he realised it, he'd be all hers.

Not that she didn't like Ralf. But his existence seemed to interfere with that of Carl's. She felt that in some way Carl was diminished because of him. Not quite original. Yet she knew she'd think the same of Carl if it were Ralf she was in love with. However that wasn't the way. Carl had the spark meant for her and Ralf didn't.

She let them get on with their work.

*

Julia cycled down Elmwood Avenue and passed Starbucks, sticking an imaginary finger in the air, before stopping and leaning her bicycle against the outside wall of Caffe Aroma. She went inside and ordered a latte. The staff nodded at her. She was a familiar sight, usually meeting up with Laura who worked there some afternoons. One of them called through into the back and Laura emerged with panini-dust on her fingers. She told Julia to wait outside, before re-

229

turning to the back room and cleaning herself up.

Julia sat in a metal chair on the outside patio, overlooking Bidwell Parkway. It was Farmers Market day and the place was heaving. Julia watched the hustle and bustle before her, wondering if she'd spot anyone she knew in the crowds. Just as that morning, when she had observed the twins for a few moments before announcing her presence, she liked to watch people without them knowing they were being watched. They seemed more real that way, without adopting any kind of persona for her benefit. She preferred people to be pure.

Laura came and sat down beside her. She was holding a glass of wine and a Cajun chicken wrap.

"So what's up?"

"Nothing much." Laura took a bite out of her wrap and continued talking. "I finish work at five. What are you up to?"

"Nothing much either. Just tried to get the twins to take me out for a drive, but there was nothing doing."

Laura laughed. "You need to take me along with you."

"Why's that?"

"One of them fancies me. I'm sure of it. They were here during the week, Wednesday I think it was, and one of them was looking at me funny. As though he were about to say something."

Julia sipped her latte, looking at Laura's eyes over the lip of her cup. "Which one?"

Laura laughed again. "You tell me," she said, "they both look the same to me."

Julia forced a smile. "You make it sound like they're Chinese."

Laura bit into her wrap again. A sliver of chicken made its

way out of the tortilla and slid down the left hand side of her chin. She wiped the snail-trail mark with her napkin.

"You don't have to worry," she said. "I'll check with you first before I sleep with one of them."

Julia looked back towards the farmer's market. She had never told Laura about her obsession, but she guessed it was somehow obvious. She sipped her coffee again. The day was bright. It felt like a day of happenings, yet at the same time there was something quiet about it.

She wasn't religious, but sometimes she thought that the act of praying might make the impossible conscious. To allow the possibility that something might happen seemed better than assuming it would never happen.

"Which one?" she said again.

"I told you, I don't know which one."

"I don't mean that. I mean which one do you think I fancy?"

Laura laughed again. She washed down the last of her wrap with the wine. "I just told you. I dunno. They both look the same to me."

*

The following Saturday Julia headed up Colvin avenue again. The weather had turned slightly. Big drops of rain hit the wooden-roofed buildings like the percussion section of a deaf orchestra. She turned her bike straight into their drive and whizzed under the cover of the upturned garage roof. The squeak of brakes on wet tyres disturbed the twins. Even in the split second that they were

231

distracted, Julia could tell that Carl was the one standing closest to her.

"Hi again."

"Hi."

"Watcha doing today?"

Carl gesticulated towards the object on the worktop. "As before," he said.

Julia flicked her eyes over to the corner. The first object stood there, buffed silver and gleaming. The object on the worktop was only halfway identical. Same shape and size, but yet to be perfected. She knew there was an analogy between Carl and Ralf just waiting to be explored, but for the moment she pushed it out of her mind and said: "So, you got a name for this yet?"

Ralf grinned. "Sure have," he said. "It's the Penguin Fu Fat Machine."

Carl grinned too. "Yep," he said, "that's what it is alright."

Julia sighed. She suddenly realised she was still straddling her bike, her feet touching the floor on tiptoes both sides. She spun one leg over the handlebars, and leant the bicycle up by the wall.

She was used to the twin's talking in their own language, although they did it less now than when they had all been growing up together. The words meant nothing at all, yet they also meant everything. She wasn't going to take any nonsense now.

"Explanation please."

Carl was the first to speak, beating Ralf by a whisker.

"Spam."

"An email?"

Ralf nodded. "The title of an email I got. It just seemed to fit."

"So it's meaningless?"

The twins shook their heads simultaneously. Carl spoke: "No. It *was* meaningless. Now it has meaning."

Julia swept a hand through her hair. "You sure about that?"

"Sure as sure," Ralf said.

"So what will it do?"

The twins looked at each other. Julia could almost feel something pass between them. Carl didn't need to shake his head to indicate that he didn't want to tell her, but Ralf overrode his decision and they went with it anyway. It was still a few moments before either of them spoke, then Carl shrugged his shoulders and spoke in a low voice: "We're going over the falls."

*

Julia had only been up to Niagara once in her life. She had taken the trip with her parents when she was close to ten. It had horrified and bored her. The noise was tremendous—both from the water and from the tourists. In a way, each was as never-ending and fluid as the other, and she wasn't sure which of them repulsed her the most. But once the shock of it passed her, all she wanted to do was to go home. Her parents were amazed. Everyone loves the falls. Julia didn't.

Her chat with the twins had left her equally shocked, but not in the least bored. She knew she couldn't talk them out of it, once they had decided to do something then they did it. However ridiculous or pointless it might be. She even thought of reporting it, but knew that would sideline her. She couldn't isolate herself from Carl. He was all she wanted and all she had.

A couple of times she called in on Laura but she couldn't convince herself to let her know what was happening. Instead she did some research online. She'd heard of the stories, of course, but was still surprised that only fifteen people had ever been known to make the attempt. And a third of those had died. Carl and Ralf had no ready answer to that one.

"It's just something we've decided to do."

"But you could get yourselves killed."

"It's just something we've decided to do."

Charles Stephens was the third to go over the falls and the first to die. In 1920 he got inside an oak barrel and strapped an anvil to his feet for ballast. When the barrel hit the water at the base of the falls the anvil kept going, breaking through the bottom lid and taking Stephens with it. His right arm was discovered still strapped in.

George Stathakis suffocated when his barrel got stuck at the back of the falls and wasn't recovered for fourteen hours. It didn't lighten Julia's mood to know that some of the other deaths weren't barrel-related—someone had gone over in a kayak, and although Robert Overacker's parachute was released correctly after he went over in a jet-ski it wasn't properly tethered to his back. Julia knew those fatalities all had two things in common. The victims were both stupid and dead.

"We want a piece of immortality," Ralf had explained.

"There's no twins been over the falls before," Carl said. "There's been a co-ed team, but not twins."

Julia left their house in a faintly concealed rage. She wanted her piece of immortality too. She wanted a baby with Carl.

234

*

Julia had been an only child, and one with a constant sense of loss. Whether at school, at home, or at Niagara, she knew there should always have been someone with her. As a kid this meant a constant nagging for a brother or sister which—as an adult—led to the desire for a child. She knew it wasn't the normal maternal instinct. It was something deeper than that. And then she'd discovered the existence of her vanished twin.

Of course she couldn't prove it, but she knew it all the same. She'd researched twins when she realised that she was falling in love with one of the kids she'd grown up with. Carl Delaney. She wanted to know whether being a twin gave him any disabilities at all, made him something other than a normal person apart from the physicality of his brother. She discovered the term for a foetus which dies in uteri in a multi-gestation pregnancy. A vanished twin. Something partially or completely reabsorbed by the mother. According to the research it could occur as frequently as one in eight pregnancies. Leaving no detectable trace at birth or before, it probably wasn't even known in most cases. Some hypotheses went on to speculate that children born in such a pregnancy may have some memories of their vanishing twins, and may feel lonely because of this. Julia felt sure it was more than speculation. She believed it to be true.

So it was imperative that Carl survive the falls, unless she could change his mind. He knew it was not only dangerous, but illegal. He knew the possibilities of drowning. And the $500 fine certainly wouldn't deny them their snatch of fame. But Julia needed to be made whole again. And in doing so, she had to tell him how she felt.

*

Julia held Laura's hand as they got off the bus and walked up Colvin Avenue. It wasn't going to be easy to separate Carl from Ralf but she had to tell him how she felt. If he didn't know then what was to stop him from killing himself. He wasn't stupid. Neither of them were. It was just that sometimes their collective zeitgeist seemed to work against them.

She remembered watching them one time at school when they went through a stage of getting bullied. Ralf had been in the middle of a group of older boys, getting pushed from one to the other like a basketball. Carl had seen it happening and ran up to the group, but instead of trying to stop it he had allowed himself to be admitted within the circle, and both of them had been pushed around together. It was as though there was an intrinsic desire for whatever happened to the one to happen to the other. This was the source of the fear within Julia now. That she wouldn't be able to find a way to loosen that bond.

She nudged Laura's ankle as she began to giggle when they reached the garage. Could the woman not take anything seriously? Then they were both leaning against the side of the building, watching Carl and Ralf put the finishing touches to their machine.

Both sections were on the workbench now, with a piece of metal soldered between them so that the two barrels together resembled the sides of a catamaran. The openings to the barrels faced them, and Julia could see they had padded and reinforced the insides with some kind of spongy-material. Could it really be enough to protect them? Suddenly she realised they'd have to be curled up whilst inside their barrels. From their positioning and the way that the machine was constructed it was inevitable that she saw the object as representing a womb. Would they be born together at the end of the drop, or would they be dead?

Feeling sick with anticipation she said her usual hello. Carl was standing nearest to her, but he didn't seem quite so shy today. She wondered if it was because Laura was with her. Safety in numbers, perhaps. She also wondered which one Laura thought had fancied her. It wouldn't matter to Laura, either would do, but it did matter to her.

Julia nodded towards Carl. "Can I talk to you for a minute?"

Before the twins had time to object, Laura eased her way further into the garage. "She means alone," she said; then patted the side of the barrel and added, "Now, aren't you going to tell me what this is all about?"

Julia almost reached out to hold his hand as they went up the steps into the back of the house, but she knew it was too much too soon. She held the door open for him as if it were her own property, the place she had lived in next door before her mother had died and her father had sold up and moved away. She'd never forgiven her mother for absorbing her twin into her own body. It had all come out during one otherwise bright summer's day just before they realised her mum had cancer. Her timing was impeccable, in retrospect; but she could never convince herself to take the accusation back.

She leant with her back against the kitchen table, watching

237

as he mooched around the room, glancing out of the window in case he could see his brother in the garage. She knew they were rarely apart. If she ever had a moment it was now.

"I'm going to talk straight," she said. "I don't want you going over the falls. You'll get killed."

His eyes narrowed. She felt sure he knew she'd asked him inside for this.

"So what's it to do with you?" he said.

"Well, we're friends aren't we?" Julia felt herself faltering. *Fuck it.* "No. No, it's more than that." She eased herself away from the table and walked towards him. He took a few steps backwards before hitting the wall behind him. Julia kept going. She reached out for his hand. Took it in hers. Looked into his eyes.

"I love you," she said.

She stood on her tiptoes and kissed him. There was no resistance, but the simple intimation of all the passion that would come. The passion that was due to her.

"I love you," she repeated. Her heart was beating as strong as the sun on a hot day. "I love you Carl."

"I'm Ralf," he said.

And in that moment she saw he was right, and her hands fell to her sides.

*

It was on October 24th that Julia found herself riding between the twins in their pick-up, the Penguin Fu Fat Machine under tarp blowing in the breeze behind them, as they drove the twenty-three miles to the falls. They hadn't chosen the day at random, it was precisely one hundred and ten years since the first attempt to go over the falls in a barrel had been made. Surprisingly it had been a woman. And a sixty-three year old at that. Annie Taylor. She had used an oak barrel with inflated pillows and a mattress for comfort, and had been fished out bruised and shaken after falling roughly 170 feet over the middle of the falls. Reportedly she had said, *No one ought ever do that again.*

Julia wasn't sure why she was with them. Whilst she held a camera in her hands, she knew there'd be plenty of others there to take photos when the time came. Every two seconds, one million gallons of water plummeted over Niagara Falls - and every month, on average, a similar number of tourists turn up to see the spectacle. Maybe she was there just to see them come out of it alive. Maybe she'd have to drive their pick-up home.

It was four months since she'd declared her love to the wrong man and as far as she knew he hadn't told anyone. She hadn't asked Laura what had happened in the garage either. Sometimes not knowing was better than knowing. The truth was, in itself, a vanished twin.

They parked some way upriver, and she watched as the twins manoeuvred the machine off the back of the pick-up. Her instructions were very specific. Once they got inside the contraption she was to make her way to a vantage point as close to the falls as she could. She was carrying binoculars as well as the camera, although all of them knew the chances of her actually seeing them were very small. But it helped, they said, to know she was there. All she knew was that they had no way of stopping the device once it got into the water.

Bobby Leech had been the first man over the falls in

239

1911. He survived, but fifteen years later he slipped over an orange peel in Christchurch, New Zealand during a lecture tour, and died from complications arising from the fall. Some references had it as a banana peel, but in Julia's mind she couldn't see that it mattered. Maybe you didn't need to fall 170ft to die, but only 6ft. That was how she had to tackle it. It wasn't the fall that killed him, but the landing.

She kissed both brothers before they entered the machine, not making a distinction between them. Truth was she was no longer sure any more. All her realities were being stripped away. She could feel loneliness at the base of her spine once more.

*

By the time she reached her vantage point they had already gone over. Everyone seemed to know something and everyone seemed to know nothing. Police helicopters searched from the sky. Everyone getting a piece of the twins to talk about to their grandchildren, to pass their fame by association down through all their assorted histories. Julia saw several pregnant women in the crowd. How many of them were carrying twins, or more? How many of them would absorb the unknown back into their bodies, bearing children forever punished to be lonely. She suppressed the thoughts, craned her neck over the side of the safety barrier, and looked despairingly into the water. There was nothing to see. Despite the sheer wonder of it all.

Caravan of Souls

Some days, when the light was just right, you could see clear out to the horizon, to such a thin line of hazy distance, that the sea and the sky became the same, a membranous bubble which circled the earth. Within that bubble, everything was contained, made safe.

But on other days, when the cloud came down to the sea and the water was prickled with rain, when the skies were rent asunder by thunder and lightning, you realised that the bubble was a façade, that external forces would always prevail, that the existence you wished to enclose yourself within could never be realised. That there would always be something other, pressing down, defeating.

Max took over ownership of the caravan park in the spring of 2009. It was a good spot, a good time to start. Despite having no direct experience—he had previously run a bar—he hadn't expected it to be difficult. And he was proven right. Many of the caravans were privately owned, so there was nothing to do but patrol them. For the others, taking bookings over the phone or the net was simple. He kept good records. Cleaning the amenities block,

241

mowing the grass, these things were simple.

Abandoned boats littered the marshes. Flip-flops were buried in the dunes. The landscape took back as much as it gave. Blakeney had none of the seaside razzamatazz indicative of other towns, it had more. Even in the height of summer it held its solitude.

Max used to sit in the wooden building at the entrance to the park, often reading, or looking out of the window. It was a quiet existence. It remained quiet for some time. So quiet that he began to look around for other things to do. Around this time, he met Alison.

He first saw her running across the main road from the chip shop. Sitting down at the quay she threw white pieces of fish to the seagulls whose cries screamed seaside. She was wearing a light cotton flower-patterned skirt, a yellow halter top, her shoulders covered by a white cardigan. Her long brown hair curled in the sea air. Later, he would watch her brush out those curls every morning only for them to re-appear in the evening. As her feet clipped the tarmac, outrunning cars, Max realised she would be his summer love. Perhaps, even, beyond that.

The rigging of boats sang as he sat beside her. A polystyrene tray of freshly-cooked chips held in his palm. He slipped and half the contents slid forwards, falling into the sea like potato-lemmings. She turned and smiled, and although it wasn't planned the ice had been broken. They exchanged a few words. He pinched a few of her chips. When she stood, he steadied her. Within days, they were kissing.

The spate of suicides followed shortly afterwards.

"Have you seen this?" Alison held the paper out to him.

242

He'd seen it but hadn't read it.

He was non-committal, feigned interest because Alison held more humanity.

"Dreadful, isn't it?" He read a few lines more. "Just walked into the sea? That's quite a way considering the low tides here."

"Exactly." She took the paper back and re-read it, as though by doing so more of the story would reveal itself. "You have to be pretty determined to do that."

"Someone saw them?"

"From a distance. You can't do anything from a distance. You can hardly shout."

She turned into him, leant her head upon his shoulder.

"They don't know anything about her yet."

"Maybe there isn't much to know."

Alison looked up, surprised. "Maybe there is *everything* to know."

He shrugged. "It's impossible to know everything, isn't it? And surely the answers are too late."

"The word *impossible* contains *possible*," she said.

*

That Sunday she invited him to her church.

Max was reluctant for several reasons. He didn't like walking amongst gravestones, and St Nicholas' Church had them in abundance. Forcing themselves vertical out of the green earth, like moss-covered teeth, their writing illegible given the vagaries of weather and time. Their dilapidation reminded him of the permanence of death, of how it is far easier to be dead a long time

243

than it is to be alive a long time. Another reason: the churchgoers themselves. The walking dead. Those who needed something in their hearts to be able to continue living, but who didn't realise they needed it—who believed religion needed them instead.

Finally, he was an atheist. He had told Alison so, as soon as he knew her beliefs, but she had been unwilling to accept it.

Still, she had slept with him.

People are nothing but convictions.

"There's a service for her," she said.

"She wasn't even local."

"Aren't we all local, in some way?"

"Aren't we all God's children?" He couldn't help but mock her.

"God is everywhere, Max."

He snorted. "You and your imaginary friend."

Still, as a member of the local community he went. He paid his respects. He gripped Alison's hand tightly as they left the church. It was both a statement of their togetherness, but also contained the promise that she owed him for his devotion.

That night, she allowed him to undress her in the light.

"You're beautiful."

"I don't think so."

"I've yet to meet a woman who *did* think so."

He saw on her face that she would rather he hadn't met many women.

The caravan rocked as they made love.

*

As summer came children weaved in and out of the vans, running, laughing, some on bicycles which ate up the turf and gouged rivulets which later ran in the rain. Parents sat outside their caravans in deckchairs, newspapers flapping unread in the breeze, sunglasses slipping on suncreamed noses. Occasionally, families went for walks from the harbour through the marshes along the concrete mounds which led to the sea. The sky welcomed them, sat vast above the scene, validated their choice. Happy times.

The fourth suicide occurred in the last week of July. It had been particularly hot, a day when even mad dogs and Englishmen stayed in the shade. Again, like the others, a lone walk out to sea. Identification confirmed her as Margaret Sherman. The body was washed up near Wells, eight miles along the coast. Unlike the others she was local. Alison knew her. She had been part of the congregation that day Max had attended church.

They sat side by side, amongst the dunes, looking out to sea. Max had his arm around her shoulders for so long it was starting to ache. Alison's eyes were wet. No floods, just damp at the sense of loss, communion with the dead. It didn't touch him.

"Everyone carries invisible dreams around with them," she said.

"We can't help everybody. Sometimes we don't even know who needs help."

She turned to face him. "God should be as plain as the nose on your face."

"You ever thought that expression through? Just how clearly can you see your own nose?"

She shrugged off his arm. "I see it clear enough when I look in the mirror."

245

"But when you look in the mirror you don't see your self."

The wind whipped up. Blew sand across their faces and into their eyes, their hair.

"Is there a good reason why I'm with you Max?"

He smiled. "There better be."

*

The success of the summer season led him to be incautious with the accounts. He was never interested in money, having made enough from the city to sit it out in the sun. The number of owner-occupied caravans far outweighed the rented ones. So for a while he paid less attention to them. Only if a booking came in, did he check the inventory. And only, during the middle of August, did he realise there was a caravan which was marked uninhabitable.

He quizzed his cleaner, a young girl from the village who, if he didn't have Alison, he might have flirted with.

"It's always been like it," she said, tucking a strand of hair behind an ear. "Never been used as far as I know."

"Which one is it?"

He followed behind, as if she were leading him like a schoolboy into class. Rabbit droppings littered his step. He wondered the sense of open sandals. Sand permanently gritted his toes. He nodded to some of the occupants as they passed the vans, others were sleeping, getting redder in the process.

"Here." She pointed to a van at the end of the row, caught between a telegraph pole and a slab of indeterminate concrete.

The van was older than the others. Its white colouring turned cream through age. Grass covered its wooden blocks, gave it

246

the appearance of resting solely on green blades. The steps which would have led to the doorway were absent. Curtains were speckled with black mold. Disuse had let in damp.

The girl stood some way back as Max approached the van. He glanced over his shoulder, already she was looking away. The closer he got to the van the less he wanted to look inside, but he could hardly turn back without doing so. As expected, the door was locked. He bent the grass surrounding the front of the van with his feet, ants ran over his bare toes, the number 43 was painted onto a concrete slab. He decided to return when he had the key.

And yet, as he passed the van, he couldn't help but glance into one of the windows. And caught his reflection looking back.

Chilled, he quickened his step. The girl was already half-way back to the office. He caught up with her. Touched her arm. *Rebecca.*

She turned.

Light balanced on her blue eyes. Her lips were soft, open. She spoke. *Yes?*

He shook his head. *Nothing. I mean, have you finished for the day?*

She nodded, and he let her go.

*

It was clear from the records that caravan 43 hadn't been used for many years. Max wondered why. At the end of the day, it was costing him money. He could either buy a new van to put on site, or utilise the space for another owned van. He preferred those, far less paperwork, a yearly fee, no cleaning contract.

He mentioned it to Alison when she visited later that day.

She was carrying a newspaper. He couldn't read the headline upside-down.

"Haven't you got enough vans already," she said.

"Maybe, but this is business."

"Maybe there are things more important than business."

She placed the newspaper on the desk in front of him. Another body had been washed up. This time near Morston. It was presumed to be another Blakeney suicide.

"I thought people liked to throw themselves off cliffs, not wade into water."

"Don't be insensitive."

"Maybe they were trying to walk on water."

"Don't wind me up, Max."

"Sorry."

"I wish I could believe that."

He kissed her, met with some resistance.

"Why am I with you?"

"We had this discussion before."

"Sometimes I don't know if it's you who's speaking or whether it's me."

He took her to see the caravan. She stood on tip-toe to peek inside.

"It's filthy."

"It's been neglected. I'll never salvage it. Would be easy to knock it down and put a new one in its place."

"I can see a pack of cards."

Max placed his face close to hers. "So there is."

"And over there, look into the kitchen. There's a box of

248

Rice Krispies."

"And . . . ?"

"And see that mug on the table. *Best Mum In The World.*"

"You can get those anywhere."

"Max, you're not really seeing what I'm seeing. This isn't one of *your* vans, this one must belong to someone. You can't just knock it down."

They took a walk amongst the dunes. Sand flicked up from Alison's trainers, described an arc, then found anonymity again. Wisps of white cloud patterned the sky. Half-way through the afternoon Alison tied her hair into a pony-tail. She ran ahead, laughing.

"Catch me!"

Max followed, the sand shifting under his feet, invading his sandals, until it seemed like he was running on water.

She allowed him to catch her. They fell down onto the dunes, eyes sparkling, mouths reaching together for a kiss. She pushed his hand away as he touched her breast. *Not here.* They kissed again, rolled onto their backs, regarded the sky.

"Don't you think it's easy to believe," she said.

"I think it's easier to disbelieve."

"Don't you *want* to believe?"

"I think wanting to believe is all that there is."

"But creation," she picked up a handful of sand and let it run through her fingers, "don't you see how marvellous it is?"

A woman walked passed, startling them with her silent steps.

"I see it's marvellous. But I also see that it's terrible," Max said.

"Do you ever forget who you are?"

"Never."

"I do." Alison sat up, looked in the direction of the walking woman. "Imagine I'm her. Imagine she's going to walk into the sea and imagine we just watch her. What do you think to that?"

Max was looking into the sun. He shielded his eyes. "I think that we're all observers at heart."

They watched as she neared the edge of the water.

"I really think she's going to do it."

"You think too much."

The figure, distant by now, bent down, picked something up, stood, skimmed a stone over the water.

*

That night, Max had a dream. He was under water, watching the rippling sun through the waves. For a moment he panicked, then breathed. He could do so. He was lying on the sea bed, just a few feet below the surface. His nostrils collected sediment in the tide.

He closed his eyes and could still see the residue of the sun; a triumvirate: as a memory, as a retina-burn, and through his eyelids. It was then that he realised someone was with him.

"Don't turn to look, I am here."

"God?" The word seemed ludicrous on his lips, the water washed it away.

"I was expected on earth, so here I am."

The water became choppy, Max realised it was caused by the movement of feet. People were walking into the sea.

"So, why all this misery," he found himself saying.

250

"I will tell you what happened."

Max waited. When the voice came again it was in his head, not voiced through water.

"For a week I invented everything and on the seventh day I rested. You're taught as much in your Sunday Schools. But what they didn't tell you is that whilst I was resting I slept. And I dreamt."

"You *created* on the seventh day?"

Water rushed into Max's ears like the draining of an immense pool. He awoke. It was raining.

He didn't reveal his dream to Alison, but afterwards he had visions.

The first was inconsequential, a memory of it happening. He only understood it had been a vision when he realised it wasn't real. The second time, he was more observant.

He stood on the dunes. It was the last week in August. Some would say the last opportunity. He scanned the shoreline. It wasn't a bucket and spade beach, painters came here more than children. There were other places along the coast for them. He had seen some of the paintings, none of them were particularly distinct.

In the distance, he saw what he was looking for. A lone figure skimming stones into the water. She had her back to him. He watched as she slipped off her flip-flops, began walking into the sea.

She wore a flower-patterned dress. He raised binoculars to his eyes, and could see the white marks on her shoulder blades adjacent to her dress straps, indicative of other clothes on other days.

She continued to walk. The sea melded her clothes around

251

her, hugged her as if a second skin. Until she was up to her neck he thought she might swim, then realised how preposterous that was. Her head descended below the waves. Max continued to watch. Some time later, she came out again.

She didn't seem any less real. She walked passed her flip-flops on the beach, headed up the dunes towards the caravan park. As she came closer, he realised it wasn't Alison. Realised he wouldn't have stopped her if it might have been.

He kept his gaze upon her until she entered the caravan. The door opened easily in her grip, although he knew it wouldn't open in his.

Lowering the binoculars he slumped onto his knees; pressing, compacting the sand.

*

Alison came with the paper the following day.

"Another death," she said.

Max barely recognised her. He had spent the night in caravan 43. The smell of damp, the stink of sea, remained in his nostrils. The sound of the waves resounded in his ears. His skin, normally smooth, was faintly sticky. His vision had yet to focus. It was as if souls became blurred in death, yet took this knowledge with them.

He rubbed his eyes. Grains of sand irritated his retina.

"You okay?"

He pulled Alison close. Felt her clothing, smelt her hair. Was this real?

You okay?

252

It was an echo, from somewhere far away. He was slipping backwards, falling, falling beyond himself.

Max?

"Max!"

An arm reached out, clutched him back. A hand stroked his hair.

"Alison?"

"Of course, who else would it be?"

He felt himself shaking his head.

At that moment, he didn't know any more.

It was only on some days, when the light was just right, that everything became clear.

Snap Shot

Is there any way to fully grasp another's story
without actually being them?
– Arlen Ford in *From the Teeth of Angels* (Jonathan Carroll)

A small, bitter man. That's Tony Henderson. His pursed lips show disdain. His achievements: a broken marriage, an unseen daughter , a slew of failed jobs. Detritus is strewn in his wake as though he's hauled a suitcase with a faulty clasp through thirty-eight wasted years.

There's nothing I know which is good about him.
One other thing: he's me.

*

Tony looked around at the large open office. Another dead end job. Plastic plants dotted the room. Computer terminals decorated with Post-it notes, fluffy animals, loved ones. His colleagues wore headsets, trapped in soulless conversations. Bite-size life. He knew

254

he would hate it there.

Cathryn smiled at him.

"This will be your desk. Gary's your team leader, but he's on a course today so we'll sit you with David. Do you want coffee, tea, water?"

He asked for water, and watched as she walked over to the cooler. She wore a tight black skirt, and a pink woollen cardigan over a white blouse. All very typical.

He thanked her when she returned, but the smile had slipped and she was distant. Tony knew he'd only got the job because the successful candidate had changed his mind. He'd been recalled at the last minute. Second best, as it were.

"Here's David."

Tony feigned interest as introductions were made. Time to reinvent himself again. Just how much would he reveal? Everyone wanted a piece of someone, but he had nothing left to give.

*

When I got home I took the chicken bhuna ready-meal out of the freezer, slipped it from its cardboard sleeve, and repeatedly stabbed the plastic cover. It was not as satisfying as breaking the seal on a coffee jar, but it released some tension.

It hadn't been a great day, but no worse than I'd expected. David was broad and sweaty. His moustache was too small. We were taking incoming calls and running through insurance quotes. Nothing different to what I was used to. Riveting stuff.

The big bonus was that calls were inbound only. And if today was typical then it wasn't busy. David had spent a third of the

255

day training me, a third answering calls, and a third flicking through *What Car?* magazine.

I'd need something to read to get through the day. There was no paperwork with the job, everything was emailed through to the back office. Off-phone time was your own. Whilst my meal heated, I ran my hand along the books on my shelf, picked something at random.

I spent the evening listening to Amy MacDonald. The flat was cold and I tucked my legs up underneath me on the sofa. My daughter used to sit like that. I tried not to wonder where she was.

*

There wasn't much to look at in the office. Tony's immediate team had little to say to each other. Apart from one girl, the rest were men. He was grateful for the lack of camaraderie. It absolved him from being sociable.

Unlike the office, the staff room was vibrant and difficult to remain anonymous. Questions chipped away at his private life, and he responded tersely whilst slowly eating his sandwiches. There was nowhere else to go. The office was on an industrial estate, even in the summer sitting outdoors wasn't an option.

The only person of interest was Katie. Small, mousey-brown hair, a little hung back from the rest. There was something about her, but he wasn't going to give himself up. There was little point in even glancing.

After a couple of days training, and a further two days trying to appear busy when it was obvious there was nothing to do, Tony put his newspaper aside and picked up his book. He'd read some Wilbur Smith before, and had bought *A Time To Die* second-hand at the Strand bookstore in New York. He'd sought refuge in the store whilst Tina had shopped for clothes. They'd flown the Atlantic in an effort to save the marriage, but it would be the last holiday either of them could afford.

The store had eighteen miles of shelving, but Tony didn't need that much choice. Grabbing the Smith he left and spent two hours asleep in the hotel room until Tina returned, laden with purchases that he spent four months paying for.

Now his headset buzzed and he took a call. Made a sale. Felt neither worse nor better for it. The book felt substantial in his hand. He turned it over and read the blurb on the back. When he opened it, the photograph fell out.

*

I don't know which came first. The revelation that I was looking at my future or at my past. The photo was so ridiculous that I knew I would make something of it. Provide some amusement for my colleagues. And also the knowledge I'd owned it unknown for three years held me fast. It was only natural, wasn't it, to find fascination in the obscure?

*

Tony turned the photograph over. The only mark was a date-stamp: *Nov 79*. A leaflet had also fallen out of the book. It was a short religious pamphlet, a single sheet of paper folded in three to make a booklet. He put it to one side.

257

The girl couldn't have been older than eleven, about the age his daughter had been when he last saw her. So, if she was eleven in 1978, she must be the same age as him now.

Tony slipped the photo back in the book, put his phone on *busy*, and went to get a drink of water. Katie was at the cooler. Suddenly he had the urge to tell her, to share the experience and create a bond between them. But he held back. He wasn't ready for it.

"You okay?"

She smiled. "Fine."

He waited patiently as her plastic cup filled, then watched her walk over to her desk. She spoke to her team leader as she sat down, and Tony fought the notion that she'd spoken about him. He half-filled a cup, drank from it, filled it again and returned to his desk.

Another call came through. He had to wait ten minutes before viewing the photograph again.

She wasn't remotely pretty. Gangly, straw-colour pigtails, teeth needing braces; yet smiling, as though she didn't know it yet. She wore a kind of traditional dress, although Tony couldn't identify which culture it represented. A white, red-speckled top. A long skirt down to her ankles. Her hands clasped in front of her. There was a gypsy-like, Romanian feel to the pic, but it was certainly American, and whilst the costume wasn't remotely Amish, it held the same religious slant which suggested the clothes were a lifestyle, not fancy dress.

Tony rubbed his finger along the top of his PC and accumulated the remains of Blu-Tack. He rolled it between his fingers, made it pliable, and then broke it into two pieces. Adhering it to the back of the photograph he stuck it against the partition separating him from David. Now all he needed was a history.

*

At the end of my shift that day I brought the photograph home and scanned it into my computer. I drank some whiskey, did an internet search on traditional American costume, but the results were either too specific or not specific enough.

The New York trip had been a disaster from start to finish, the final nail in the marital coffin, and somehow—knowing I'd brought this image home with me—the photograph felt a signifier of something new. It didn't matter that almost thirty years had passed since it was snapped: it pre-dated and foreshadowed all the same.

A Time To Die was published in 1989, ten years after the photograph was taken. There was no relevance for it being in the book other than for me to find it.

I wondered what the girl was doing now. What she would think if she knew I had this photograph. I wondered who would have put it in the book. As the whiskey burnt my throat I knew I was raising more questions than answers. And that I wouldn't find the answers. The route of obsession was a long and empty road.

I picked up the phone and tried to call Tina, but she'd changed her number again.

*

"That's Melody."

259

David peeled the photograph from the partition and looked at it closely.

"Who's she then?"

"My girlfriend."

"Looks a little young to be your girlfriend." He sounded nervous, as though part of him thought Tony was capable.

"That's an old photograph, as you well know. She's nearly forty now."

David shrugged. Tony knew he was wondering, *Why that old photograph. Why not something recent.*

"Say, what's that?"

It was Katie.

"This is Melody. Tony's girlfriend."

David handed the photo over. Katie held it up to her face, squinting as though it were framed in gauze.

"Where's she from?"

"The States," Tony said. "That was taken a long while ago, of course. It's the oldest photo I have of her."

"I see." Katie handed the photograph back.

David gave Tony a look which was just the civil side of disparaging.

Smugly, Tony reaffixed the photo to the partition.

A story developed. Melody had come over to the UK with her parents in 1990 when she was twenty-one. She had studied at Cambridge, but gradually distanced herself from her family until she rescinded their religious beliefs, skipped out of college, and worked for a year in an Israeli kibbutz. That's where Tony had met her, picking dates and bananas. They'd had a short but intense romance, breaking up when Tony returned to the UK.

He'd had no contact with her for fifteen years, in between he got married—he left out any mention of his daughter—and following his divorce he'd received a postcard from her out of the blue and they'd met up again.

This was how he told it to Cathryn, who had been the first to ask the background. The façade of polite interest she had at the start of the conversation turned to warmth as she heard how Tony and Melody got back together. Even so, he could tell she found the choice of photograph puzzling, so he tweaked the story after a few days to add that it was the only photo he had of her. She was camera shy to the point of being camera phobic. Didn't believe in capturing the soul. That made everything simpler.

Tony knew it was only a pathetic game of one-upmanship, but it made him smile. Fuck them. Fuck them all.

*

I switched off the car headlights as I turned into Tina's road, slowly cruised until I was opposite her new address before parking.

A light was on in an upstairs room, presumably a bedroom. I wondered if she was alone. It didn't bother me. She could see whoever she wanted. All I wanted was my daughter.

She had almost screamed down the telephone. *What bastard gave you this number?* All the usual stuff. I kept calm. You know what I want. *I don't want to see you.* What did you do to her? She hung up.

My daughter could have gone to university. I watched the bedroom light until it became too cold to sit in the car. As I turned at the bottom of the road I saw the light wink out behind me.

Back at my flat I posted the photograph under the heading

Do you know this girl? on several American online message boards. Then I did my usual round up of reading the replies I'd already had. Most of them were comical, denigrations of the ugly child, typically nasty stuff from nasty people. But there were always a few with compassion, and not infrequently from men who I felt were missing something in their own lives. Perhaps they too had a child that was no longer with them. Who needed the comfort of strangers to get through the night.

I'd made it as honest as possible: *Found in Wilbur Smith's* A Time To Die *bought at the Strand bookstore, New York. Image has* Nov 79 *stamped on the back. Interested in returning to the rightful owner.* Plus my email address.

There was no point in complicating things.

*

In the next team meeting Gary informed them that they were going to introduce bi-monthly after work bonding sessions. It wasn't compulsory, but it was. "It's just a bit of fun," Gary said, as though no one could possibly object to a bit of fun.

"Any suggestions?"

The consensus was bowling.

Clive, slightly older than the rest and who Tony disliked because he had a very attractive wife sitting in a gold-rimmed frame on his desk, brought up the subject of partners.

"Sure," Gary said. "Why not? Any objections?"

Tony was the first out of the room.

At lunch time Katie was alone in the staff room when Tony entered. She was watching *Loose Women*, but the daytime show didn't suit her. It was written all over her face. She wanted to talk.

"You okay Tony?"

"I'm fine."

"I'm not keen on this new idea, are you? This bonding thing. It's too intrusive."

Tony nodded.

It all came out in a rush.

"I mean, if we wanted to socialise with each other we'd do it, wouldn't we? We shouldn't be made to do it. It's embarrassing. They'll all have their partners there too."

Katie twisted her fingers through a loop of hair that hung around her shoulders.

"Maybe we should boycott it," Tony said. "Or maybe we should go together."

She laughed. "Yeah, right. Not sure your Melody would be so keen on that."

Tony chewed slowly.

"She'd be fine."

Katie smiled. "Sure she would."

"Really, she'd be fine."

Katie glanced at the door.

"Do you love her?"

"Pardon?"

"Just seems a little strange that you're offering to take me on a date, that's all."

Tony coughed. "Hardly a date, is it."

"Isn't it?"

*

263

At home I used her photograph as my screensaver. I came to like that big toothy smile even though it was the antithesis of all that I found beautiful.

I'd tentatively kissed Katie only that morning, three months after starting work, and eighty-six days after finding the photograph, when the first email arrived in my inbox titled: *It's me!*

Hey! Just browsing the net and I came across the photo! That was me! Some crazy costume, huh? Tell me more about where you found it. Corinne.

I ran a hand through my hair. Was this genuine? A month ago I'd been relentlessly spammed by a religious fanatic who had become obsessed that I'd posted the photo for paedophile purposes. But I'd changed my email since then, and this was hardly in the same vein. What would I do?

I downed some whiskey and wrote a reply. Tried to be as upbeat as possible, queried what career path she had taken and asked a few open-ended questions. When I clicked *send* I realised I didn't know if this was the beginning or the end.

I switched off the PC and watched a rerun of *Rebus*. The phone sat quiet in the corner. I hated to think that the only reason I would ever want to contact Tina would be to quiz her about my daughter. There should be more to it than that.

Then, before I went to bed, I turned the PC back on and read Corinne's reply.

*

The day after Tony had the conversation about the bonding sessions with Katie in the staff room he had pinned up a new photo of Melody on his board. It was bad timing. Katie had certainly voiced her interest, but the temptation to take the charade further proved too much.

Cathryn saw it first. As the floorwalker she was more mobile than most of them.

"So this is her now? Thought you said she didn't like having her picture taken?"

"I persuaded her otherwise. Told her the reaction her younger self had been getting." The smile might have been fixed on Tony's face with Blu-Tack itself.

Cathryn leant in for a closer look. Tony could smell her perfume.

"She's come on a bit, hasn't she?" Cathryn laughed. "I'm only joking. I think she's lovely."

"Improved with age," Tony said.

During the course of the morning Gary, David, and the rest of the team also took a look. As did Katie when she passed by on her way to the cooler. Tony gave her a pained smile loaded with double-meaning.

"Don't think putting up a new photo means you don't have to bring her bowling," David said.

The story continued: when she'd left the kibbutz she'd wanted to track Tony down, but her address book had been amongst belongings stolen by a pickpocket in Bethlehem. Tony had tried to write via the kibbutz, but for reasons neither of them had been able to fathom his letters hadn't been forwarded. *Maybe someone was jealous*, laughed Melody. So they'd drifted apart and led

265

separate lives, although Melody had remained single and vowed that she would never marry until she stumbled across Tony again.

The internet had proved crucial in finding him. Late one night, bored with chatrooms, Melody had searched Facebook. It was the first anniversary of Tony's divorce, and the coincidence seemed prescient. Within twenty-four hours they were back together. Just as it was meant to be.

*

Corinne sent me a photograph. Unlike the image I'd found of Melody online, this one was more of a match. I flicked back and forth, between 1979 and 2009, and the resemblance was obvious. She hadn't exactly *improved with age*, but there was a warmth and honesty in her face that hit home.

She was single. Still living in America—she'd never left it—had almost married once, but the engagement never came to anything. She seemed as interested in me as I was in her, and late at night, a third of the way through a bottle of Jack Daniels, it struck me how stunning it would be to follow this through to its logical conclusion.

I swilled the whiskey in my glass. Forget all that reality which everyone douses themselves in, which makes them feel unique and individual, forget all that crap. The set of coincidences forced into collusion for me and Corinne to meet were breathtaking. We had to get together. Even if all that followed were shit, it would be the most avant-garde singular spur of the moment thing I'd ever done. Just thinking about it made my heart beat faster.

Our email communications grew, gained emotional depth, connections formed and gelled between us.

*

Tony watched the front of the building as Katie left work. He flashed his lights and she headed over. She was wearing a dark blue trouser suit which was too businesslike for her, as though she were pretending to be someone else. Tony stroked his day-old stubble with his right hand, then cupped his palm and blew into it. His heater was on the blink.

She opened the car door and slipped inside.

"Hi."

"Hi, you."

She leant over and brushed her lips against his.

"Bit risky, innit?"

"I don't care what those arseholes think."

Her giggle was suddenly irritating. Tony realised it was too easy.

He turned on the radio. Chris Evans filled the car. Katie wound down the window and lit a cigarette, the smoke mingling with her icy breath.

"You're a dark horse you are."

"How'd you mean?"

"They say the quiet ones are the worst."

Tony shrugged. "Takes all sorts."

"I'm thinking of leaving." Katie flicked the ember through the open window and turned to face him. "It's stifling here. I don't know how you can stand it. A friend says she can get me a job as a trainee manager at Grainger's. More money, more responsibility. What do you think?"

Tony thought that he wasn't interested. "You have to do what's best for you," he said.

"And it'd make things easier for us, wouldn't it?"

"Would it?"

"No sneaking around like."

"But less opportunity, surely?"

Katie delved into her handbag for another cigarette, then thought better of it.

"You need to choose between me and Melody."

Tony snorted, mucus shot out of his nose.

"Jesus, Tony!"

"Sorry." He wiped it off his trousers with a dirty handkerchief.

"Is it really that funny?" She was already halfway out of the car. He didn't answer. Just watched as she re-entered the building.

*

I continued the story at home. It seemed easier to leave Tina alone. When I returned from work it was a simple matter of preparing a quick evening meal and logging onto MSN where Corinne and I were getting acquainted. Because of the time difference we were never long together, but there was so much about us that buzzed that we could have occupied the same physical space, not separated by miles and identified only through pixels.

I began to consider travelling to the States. America was a whole new ball game. A place where the pressure of being Tony and the absence of my daughter wouldn't be so great. Corinne was going to be my salvation.

It was going to be difficult keeping up with all the lies.

Corinne, I typed. *I need to tell you something.*

Go on.

*

Monday morning Tony was late for work. His eyes were underscored by dark lines. He smelt of drink. An uneasy recognition passed between Gary and David. Smiles were cracked.

Before he had the chance to log onto his workstation Cathryn came over.

"Tony, can I just have a quick word please."

In her office, the police were waiting.

"Do you mind leaving us alone Miss Clarkson?"

She closed the door on them.

"You're a hard man to track down, Tony."

"What do you want with me?"

"Your ex-wife, Ms Tina Watts, has made an informal complaint of harassment. Now we all know what this is about—we've been here before—but I'm not going to gloss over the seriousness of this. She has good grounds to enforce the injunction against you if she wants to."

She killed my daughter.

He shook his head. "I think the position on that is clear, don't you. The inquest confirmed it was an unfortunate accident. You're doing yourself no favours by harbouring this grudge, Mr Henderson. No favours at all."

I held my head in my hands.

"We've availed ourselves of your new address through Miss Clarkson here. Should we have to pay a call on you, Mr Henderson, I fully expect you to be home in the early hours of the morning, and not within the exclusion zone detailed in the injunction order."

I could imagine all eyes on the police as they left the building.

*

Tony waited in the office until Cathryn came back.

"I suppose this is everywhere now."

"No one has to know anything other than what you tell them." Cathryn looked genuinely flustered. "For what it's worth, I remember it in the papers now. Didn't realise of course, but you have my deepest sympathy Tony."

"Sure."

"Don't be so cynical." She sat down on the corner of her desk. "I've got two kids. I couldn't bear to lose either of them. And whilst I can't begin to understand what you must have been through, I'm not so insensitive that I can't guess. Take the rest of the day off, you look like you've been through the mill anyway. We'll see you tomorrow."

Tony stood and looked across the office space. Gary and David immediately put their heads down. Katie was nowhere to be seen. No matter, he knew he wasn't coming back. America beckoned.

*

I waited fifteen minutes for Corinne to come online. She never missed our daily chat, so I shot off an email, snapped the clasp on another bottle, and then slid open my desk drawer and pulled out the photos of my daughter.

*

Tony looked up at the window. The night was cold, his fingers were clenched to keep warm. Looking around, he couldn't see his car. He couldn't remember how he got there.

*

A life cut short. She had fallen off a hotel balcony in Spain, only two stories tall but high enough to kill her. It was Tina's fault. It couldn't have been mine. Because I wasn't there.

*

The stairwell was quiet. The walls were bare concrete. Nothing more than convenience. Tony held onto the metal rails and began to ascend. He passed Katie on the way down, but they barely glanced at one another.

*

My daughter was nothing like the eleven year old in the photograph. She was beautiful, a real credit to her parents. Her eyes

271

shone with life, and though she could talk the back end off a donkey she was so full of humour you didn't give a toss.

*

Tony fished in his pocket for the key. There was a light on. The net curtains patterned the opposite wall. He quietly replaced the key in his pocket. Tried the handle. It opened.

*

She'd lived with me for three years after the divorce. When Tina got back in the picture and took some notice again she decided to whisk her off to Spain to make up for things. It took a court battle to get her there and I've been both in battle and in court ever since.

*

Tony trod carefully. Empty Jack Daniels' bottles littered the hallway. The apartment was quiet. No television, no radio, no voices. At the bottom of the hall the bedroom door was open and he could see Tina on the bed. She was reading a book. Wilbur Smith's *A Time To Die*.

*

Corinne came online. I typed a few fast sentences. *Missed you. Had a hell of a day. Really need to chat right now. I love you very much.*
I sat back and wiped my eyes.

272

*

Tony glanced in the hall mirror. Business as usual. In the kitchen, Melody was making a peanut butter sandwich.

*

A shadow fell across the computer.
I saw both myself and the truth for the very first time.

If I have not love, I am nothing
– 1 Corinthians 13:2

About the Author

Andrew lives and works in Norfolk, UK, with his poet-partner Sophie, his daughter Sarah, and the obligatory three cats.

He began writing in 1987, although his stories didn't start appearing in print until 1994, the first being "Pussycat" in the Barrington Books anthology, *The Science of Sadness*. That publication was pivotal, as the anthology heralded the new wave of 'slipstream'—a genre which Andrew realised he had been writing all along. Since that date, he's had over 80 stories published in a wide range of magazines and anthologies, but has always remained faithful to his slipstream roots, crafting fiction which touches on the edges of other worlds and possibilities, whilst remaining anchored in the present day.

Forthcoming publications include *Slow Motion Wars*, a collaborative collection of short fiction co-written with Allen Ashley (due sometime from Screaming Dreams Press). A crime novel is in edit, and he is currently writing stories for yet another collection. In the meantime, his website is andrew-hook.com.

Bibliography

The Virtual Menagerie (Elastic Press, 2002)
Moon Beaver (ENC Press, 2004)
Beyond Each Blue Horizon (Crowswing Books, 2005)
Reside (Half-Cut Publications, 2006)
And God Created Zombies (NewCon Press, 2009)
Ponthe Oldenguine (Atomic Fez, 2010)

Dog Horn Publishing presents...

a preview of Deb Hoag's upcoming novel

Chapter One
Dorothy: The Meeting

I don't know much, but I know this: magic is all around us, every day. It's in the air we breath, the water we drink. Sometimes it's wonderful, and sometimes it's absolutely horrid. Magical things are happening to all of us, all the time, without rhyme or reason, without a care in the world about who deserves it or who doesn't.

Magical things have happened to me. My name is Dorothy, and this is my story.

*

I met Frannie in the spring of 1890, the night I got thrown into the hoosegow for getting overly friendly with a couple of guys at the local saloon. I stomped into the cell and threw myself dramatically on the bunk, except it wasn't the bunk I landed on – it was another woman. I hadn't seen her there in the dim light leaking in from the booking room.

She made an 'oofing' noise and I jumped off the bed faster than I had jumped on, and the guard laughed. A small horde of adolescent jitterbugs that were prancing around on the ceiling giggled shrilly, but my mundane companions didn't notice.

"Well, excuse me," the woman said with a sniff, sitting up and putting a hand to a hairdo that had seen better days.

"Sorry, sister," I replied, scooting over to the wall, where I slid down into a sitting position.

The jitterbugs went back to their endless, intricate mating dance, having approximately the same attention span as the gnats they so closely resembled.

The tiny flashing disco light was annoying, but I did my best to ignore it. I'd learned early that people who see things no one else does get a one-way ticket to the nearest loony bin.

Even jail was better than that, which reminded me of exactly where I was. Jail. Fuck!

I thunked the back of my head against the concrete. It hurt like hell, so I did it a couple more times. Stupid, stupid, stupid getting caught like that! A few more dollars and I would have been on my way back to Kansas, chasing cyclones till I could find one that would take me back to Oz.

"Hey, honey, it can't be that bad," said the woman, eying me with alarm.

I stopped banging my head and sighed. "I was this close to going home, and I got picked up by some needle-dick copper for soliciting. Now I'm stuck here until I can see the judge, pay a fine, maybe a bribe, and then earn the money I'd saved all over again. And I'm on a deadline. I need to get back to Kansas before cyclone season hits."

She laughed. "If you can make enough money out of these hayseeds to bribe a judge, you're even better than you look. Most of these hicks would rather boink a sheep than pay money for a tumble with an actual woman."

I sighed again. Completely true. I should have known two guys with cash money in a frontier town like Aberdeen, South Dakota were too much of a good thing.

"Look," I said, "I didn't mean to sit on you. I really didn't know you were there. I'm Dorothy. I just blew into town a couple of weeks ago. Who are you?"

She shook her head sadly. "I'm Frannie, from right here. For the last few years, at least. I hale from back east, originally."

"God, you actually live in this podunk town? You poor thing."

We sat in companionable silence. Eventually, my thoughts brought me back around to what I'd been doing that landed me in jail, and from that to what my cellie had been doing that landed her in jail.

"So, what exactly got you thrown in here?"

Her face grew sulky. "I committed a lewd act in public."

"Wow. What constitutes a lewd act around here?"

She shrugged and looked annoyed. "Looking cross-eyed on a Tuesday, if the constable is in a bad mood. It wasn't really even in public. We were in a perfectly respectable alley. It just happened that the alley was behind the police chief's house, and his wife picked that very moment to look out the bedroom window."

"Gee, that sucks."

"Yes, and so did I. That's why I got arrested."

I laughed out loud. Frannie started laughing too. Just like that, I knew we were going to be good friends.

When we stopped laughing, Frannie stretched on the narrow cot and stood up. "I've got an extra blanket," she said. "It gets quite cold in here at night. You want it?"

"Sure," I said, and she walked over to drape it around my shoulders.

When she stood up, the jitterbugs' disco ball illuminated her face and figure. She had a square, short jaw, and lush, full lips. Her nose was a little large for her small face, but it lent humor to an otherwise serious visage and her eyes were beautiful and large, thickly lashed. In the dim light she was altogether pretty, and she had a grace of movement that gave her lithe frame an inviting wiggle when she moved, top-heavy the way men liked. The farmers probably ate her up. She looked closer to thirty than twenty, but I prefer older women, myself. She wore boots she must have sent all the way to New York for, and had the goodies wrapped up in a scarlet silk dress that suggested all kinds of mischief.

If I wasn't heartbroken over Glinda, that wicked bitch, I might have eaten her right up myself.

I must have been staring, because she blushed, and reached up a hand to check her hair again. Her hands were large but well-shaped, with long, sensitive fingers. When she tucked the blanket around me, I smiled up at her, and noticed an unfortunate Adam's apple, nearly as large as a ma--

Was that a wisp of mustache on her upper lip?

"Are you . . . ah, you wouldn't happen to be . . . I know this sounds crazy, but are you a man?" I blurted out, watching as her painted cheek turned even rosier than it already was.

Frannie raised one of those large hands to tidy hair I realized now was a wig, askew on her head. I reached up and gave it a tug to set it straight.

She slid down to the floor and leaned against the wall a scant distance from me.

"You've found me out. Our guard doesn't know that I sat next to him on a pew just last Sunday in a suit coat and tie. Are you going to tell him?"

"Your secret is safe with me. It's no skin off my nose."

Frannie blinked. "Really? That's a refreshing attitude. You didn't grow up around here, did you?"

"Well, I'm from Kansas, originally, but . . . "

"I've been to Kansas. I didn't realize they grew 'em so liberal there."

"Oh, Kansas isn't really my home."

"Then why do you want to get back there?"

"It's a long story."

She laughed. "Sister, time is one thing we both have plenty of, given the present circumstances."

I had to agree.

I didn't suppose for a second that she would believe a word I said, but I didn't think she'd call the local loony bin about me, either.

I nestled in more comfortably to begin my tale.

"It all started in New Orleans . . . "

More Fiction from
Dog Horn Publishing

Shark by Wes Brown
RRP: £9.99, 176pp, ISBN: 9781907133145

Yorkshire writer Wes Brown's debut novel, *Shark* is a story about the dispossessed and how they get by.

Ex-soldier and violent deadbeat John Usher returns to his boyhood home of Leeds to find things have changed. His community has been unravelled by gang culture, ethnic tensions and hopelessness. Unable to sleep, his only consolation is drinking late into the night and playing pool by himself. That is, until an encounter with a hard right activist leads him into a twisted relationship of deceit, cuckoldry and hatred.

The Bride Stripped Bare by Rachel Kendall
RRP: £9.99, 123pp, ISBN: 9781097133046

Finally bound into one collection, twenty three stories of creation and mutation. From twisted fairy tales and grubby nights to circus freaks and insect bites, these tales of depravity reveal the bride in her most scabrous form.

Hemorrhaging Slave of an Obese Eunuch by Tom Bradley
RRP: £9.99, 140pp, ISBN: 9781907133039

In the middle of the Adriatic Sea during Neronic times, in Hiroshima Cathedral's demon-infested basement, in the royal elephant stables of a Hindustani town three millennia ago, in a Tokyo AIDS hospice disguised as a derelict kindergarten, on a yacht anchored off a South China leper isolation colony, and on top of a skull-shaped and -textured geothermal formation in the prune-colored midnight.

Celebrated author Tom Bradley's latest short story collection *Hemorrhaging Slave of an Obese Eunuch* will take you to all of these places.

A History of Sarcasm by Frank Burton
RRP: £9.99, 158pp, ISBN: 9781907133015

Sometimes stories that I've used to mythologize my childhood resurface in my mind as actual memories . . . Perhaps if you tell a story enough times, it will become the truth.

This admission by Mark Greensleeves, the compulsive liar in the story 'Some Facts About Me', sums up Frank Burton's sharp, surreal and subversive short story collection, *A History of Sarcasm*. The seventeen stories in this collection blur the boundaries between fact and fantasy through a series of obsessive characters and their skewed versions of reality. Among them are a man who insists on living every aspect of his life in alphabetical order, a girl who believes she is receiving secret messages through the TV, a paranoiac who is pursued by an army of giant lobsters, and an academic who turns into a cat.

ND - #0153 - 270225 - C0 - 229/152/16 - PB - 9781907133251 - Matt Lamination